MISTLETOE

TONI BLAKE

www.toniblake.com

This is a work of fiction. Names, characters, places, and incidents are a product of the author's imagination. Locales and public names are sometimes used for atmospheric purposes. Any resemblance to actual people, living or dead, or to businesses, companies, events, institutions, or locales is completely coincidental.

Mistletoe / Toni Blake -- 1st ed.

ISBN: 978-1-943966-28-8

❀ Created with Vellum

❄

To my editor, Lindsey Faber, for getting my vision for this story, loving the book as much as I do, and helping me make it better!

CHAPTER ONE

$\mathcal{T}$he last thing Shelby Scott needed in her life was a hot, sexy man. And yet when the door opened on the pickup truck that had just pulled to the curb near her wrecked car, a hot, sexy man is exactly what stepped out. Tall, dark-haired, and a little scruffy, he'd obviously just come from putting in a hard day's work somewhere. A smudge of dirt streaked the front of his blue T-shirt and his well-worn jeans sported a rip across one knee. But none of that dimmed her instant awareness of his blue eyes, commanding jawline, or broad shoulders.

And sure, she had plenty else to worry about at the moment besides hot, sexy men, but given that the same type of man had brought her to this surreal moment in time—standing along a desolate low country South Carolina highway beside a wrecked car she couldn't afford to repair or replace—it was hard to ignore that particular quality in the guy striding toward her.

"You okay?" he asked as he drew closer.

Despite a few bumps and bruises, she nodded. "Better than the car anyway." They both spared the mid-size sedan a glance where it straddled a ditch, the hood bowed, the grille smashed against a huge old oak tree dripping with Spanish moss. A mere car had no chance against a tree with that much history.

"Looks like you went on a wild ride." Mr. Hot and Sexy motioned to the twisting black skid marks that snaked up the asphalt behind her.

"A tire blew and I lost control."

"Well, the important thing is that you're okay. Probably shook up, though. Got somebody to call?"

She blinked. Such a simple question. She wished the answer were as easy. "Not really. I'm not from around here. I was headed to a town called Sassafras."

His mouth unfurled into a gentle grin. "Almost made it, too—city limits sign is just around that bend." He pointed to a wide curve about a hundred yards away. "I can give you a lift. Where ya headed exactly?"

Shelby weighed her answer. Another question that seemed simpler than it was. Did she dare let this stranger know where she'd be staying? At the moment, she didn't want *anyone* to know—that was the whole point in coming here. But she couldn't see any other options at the moment. "Cypress Stump Road."

His nod came with a guarded expression of surprise, uncertainty. "Not much out that way."

That's why I'm hoping you're a good guy and not a bad one— since you're my only option at the moment. "It's a family place. A cottage at the end of the road."

"Well, hop in the truck and I'll drop you off."

"It's not out of your way?"

"Nah. Just outside town a few miles." Then he looked toward the wrecked vehicle. "Need anything from your car?"

Her mind spun. Thank God he'd asked or she might not have realized quickly enough. He was right—the accident had left her unsteady. Calm, though—because she'd taught herself that trait—but still not thinking as clearly as she should. Wrecking the car put a pretty big hitch in her plan and she'd have to wade through all the ramifications once she got where she was going and could regroup.

"Yes, actually—thanks." She started toward the sedan, aware as she reached for her keys that her hands were trembling. From the accident. From the change in plans. From suddenly being forced to accept the kindness of a handsome stranger. This wasn't how she'd expected her afternoon to go.

When the man walking beside her through the tall roadside grass peered down into her trunk, his eyes widened. "Wow. All this?"

The space was packed tight with boxes and bags. "Yes. Sorry. And the stuff in the backseat, too." Which was a pile of clothes on hangers, and a laundry basket filled with socks, underwear, and bras. It had seemed the easiest way to move that kind of stuff and she'd never expected anyone to see it all but her. Again, best laid plans.

"So you're gonna be here a while then," he concluded, hefting a couple of small but weighty boxes labeled *Photo Albums* and *Books* from the trunk. "Not just visiting somebody for the holidays."

Christmas was only a few weeks away, so the notion made sense—but as she grabbed up totes and shopping bags filled with towels and sheets, she confirmed what the photos and towels likely made obvious. "Moving."

"What brings you here? A...job?"

"I'll actually be looking for one," she confessed as they plodded toward his truck carrying her belongings. "I, um, wanted a new start someplace quiet. This place came for free, so...here I am."

She tried to sound cheerful about it, even adding a quick

smile, but knew the words came out stiff. Stiff enough to turn the conversation awkward as they lowered their armloads of stuff into the bed of his big 4x4 truck. She suddenly suspected that Sassafras didn't draw a lot of newcomers—or have a lot of job opportunities.

"Where ya from?" he asked as they started back to the car.

"Chicago." A part of her didn't like divulging even that. *Don't tell anyone anything*, her friend and ex-coworker Marta had warned before she left. Marta was the only person who'd even known she was leaving, the only person she'd been brave enough to trust a little. But Chicago was a big city, and far enough away that it seemed safe to share.

As they took more stuff from the trunk, Mr. Hot and Sexy laughed. "From Chicago to Sassafras—sorry to tell you, but that seems like a big step down. Not gonna find much shopping or nightlife around here. No big holiday extravaganzas or anything."

"That's fine with me," she assured him. "Like I said, I'm all about the peace and quiet."

"Well, you'll get plenty of *that*."

"You don't like it here?" she asked. An attempt to change the subject from her to him.

"Oh, I like it fine. Born and raised here. Maybe was a time I thought I'd end up somewhere else, but it didn't work out that way."

There was a story there, and she was tempted to ask about it. But she didn't. Because she hadn't come here to form relationships. She'd come here to lay low. Keep to herself. Figure out how to start over. And that didn't include trusting or getting to know anyone. And it probably wouldn't for a very long time. Fate had made her a loner—not by choice but by circumstance. She didn't necessarily *want* to be alone, but she kept ending up that way, and for right now, it was safer to just accept that.

One more load from the car—she rushed to grab up the laundry basket, along with a shopping bag of pajamas and shorts, letting him take the clothes on hangers, mostly tops and a few sundresses and casual skirts. She'd left every professional piece of apparel behind because that life was over. Well, at least for the foreseeable future.

Even in early December, the sun here was warm enough to make her glad they'd soon be out of it—and as they walked side by side, she wondered if he was noticing the bra on top in the basket she toted, its pink cups adorned with tiny rhinestones. She suspected he did, making her feel still a tad more awkward. A life that included sexy bras was over, too— but she'd brought it anyway because it was comfortable and supportive, and good bras were expensive.

As she climbed up into the passenger side of the truck, she tried to ignore how very masculine the space felt—right down to the scent. From the worn ball cap on the dashboard bearing the words Mid Carolina Speedway to the plaid flannel shirt tossed over the console to the musky smell emanating from the worn leather seats, everything inside the truck told her she was in the space of a guy's guy. She hated how drawn to that she felt—instantaneously, something chemical in her body connecting, reacting. Because at the same time it repelled her—due to recent history, and the stark fear that invoked. So she didn't get too comfortable.

And as Mr. Hot and Sexy got behind the wheel, closed his door, and the truck rumbled back onto the road, her sense of unease grew. Everything about her future had *already* loomed uncertainly, and now she'd lost the use of her car and had just accepted a ride with a stranger.

"I'm Jason Rose," he introduced himself. "But most people call me Jace."

Okay, not officially a stranger anymore. "I'm Shelby," she said. Leaving off her last name. Maybe that was silly. But

Marta's words stayed with her. *Don't tell anyone anything.* And already that was going poorly. "Thank you for the ride—I appreciate it."

"Sorry your move is getting off to a bad start," he told her. He struck her as thoughtful and polite for such a rugged guy. Downright normal, in fact. But then, Craig had once seemed normal, too.

"Thanks." Bad indeed. But she refused to belabor that. She just wanted to get to the house, get settled, then figure out what to do next.

The lonely, flat stretch of road had just given way to the edge of town, cottages and clapboard homes now lining both sides of the street—and soon they passed a few businesses, a library, a grocery store, and a gas station.

As the truck rounded a curve that brought them into a more old-fashioned part of town, now labeled Main Street, her eyes fell on a sign for The Rose Tavern. "Any relation?" she asked, again wanting to change the subject more than really wondering.

"Yeah, my older brother Rick owns the place."

She nodded, mildly surprised the answer was yes.

"Nice enough place to get a drink if you're thirsty—and has a cool mural on the ceiling his girlfriend painted." He'd slowed the truck now that they were in town, and she took note of a drugstore, hardware store, and a bank.

That quickly, though, they were back on the outskirts of Sassafras, headed in the direction of the ocean. "I can call a tow truck if you want," Jason Rose offered. "I know a good repair place they could take the car. Or maybe you want to call your insurance company first?"

Across the cab of the truck, she sighed. Another simple question, another complicated answer. "Thanks, but...I don't have insurance." A lie, but easier than the truth. *I share an insurance policy with the lunatic I just escaped from, and I can't risk them contacting him with my whereabouts.* "And I can't really afford to have it repaired right now."

She felt Jason Rose's glance from behind the wheel, but kept her own eyes straight ahead, watching the scenery out the window, the road growing rapidly more desolate again. Marshlands lined one side, and a couple of what she thought might be heron stood in the shallow water on tall, skinny legs. "That's a shame," he said. And across the cab of the truck she could feel his surprise—or maybe it was worry for her. She was a woman without a car or money or a job in a new place where she didn't know anyone. *She* probably seemed like a lunatic. Or, at the very least, a loser. "Still probably want to get the car towed, though, don't you?"

However, at the moment the car seemed a lost cause. Because of the whole insurance issue and knowing how much it cost to fix one without it. And she had some cash— enough to get started here—but she hadn't counted on having to squander some of it on towing a vehicle that had just become useless to her. Part of her wanted to just leave it there, forget it even existed. "I can't afford a tow truck, either," she finally said.

His silence made his bewilderment obvious. He was clearly not a man who abandoned cars. She'd never been a woman who would abandon a car, either—until now. This was new territory for her—figuratively and literally. There was no one to call for money. She wouldn't ask Marta for any more help than she'd already given. She wouldn't go running to her uncle, either. The point here was to get her independence back and she was going to handle this on her own—somehow.

Of course, to abandon the car was to leave...a clue. An impounded car could be traced if someone was looking for you hard enough. And surely the car was worth something even if totaled. But her brain was on overload, so this would just have to wait.

"Look," she said, suddenly feeling the need to say more, "I know this seems weird. But I'm just in a pinch financially right now. Limited funds until I get settled and find a way to make some money. Normally I'm a person who *has* insurance and *has* someone to call when she wrecks her car. Normally I'm a person who can afford a tow truck. But just not right now, so I'll have to figure out the answers later."

He stayed quiet for a moment longer as the truck crossed a low bridge over swampy land. And then he asked, "Can I help?"

She swallowed. The offer was kind. But she couldn't accept it. For so many reasons. Not wanting charity. Not wanting to owe someone. Not wanting to trust. "Thanks, but I'll be fine."

"I'm not sure how," he said.

She darted him a look, taken aback.

"I mean, this is no place to be without a car, honey." He sounded almost put out with her—maybe wondering how she'd gotten herself into such a bind. "I don't know how you're gonna look for a job without a car, or get groceries without a car, or get anywhere else without a car."

Okay—she wasn't sure of that, either, but said, "I can walk."

"It's at least a couple miles from the far end of Cypress Stump Road to Delia's Market—which is right here," he said, pointing. The dark, wooden structure—close enough to water to be on stilts—was smaller than a grocery store, but also friendlier-looking.

"Then it's fortunate I'm in good shape."

She was grateful when he didn't answer. And as they made a left turn onto what she assumed was Cypress Stump

Road, she thought maybe he was beginning to accept that she wasn't looking for help and would be just fine on her own.

Walking that far for food would be challenging, and he was right—getting and keeping a job would be ridiculously harder without transportation, too. But she'd figure it out. Maybe she'd find a clunker for sale...somehow, somewhere. She didn't have all the answers—very few, in fact, after that blown tire changed things so much—but she had faith all this would work out. Because life wasn't supposed to be this hard. She knew it would get better, more stable, with hope for a brighter future, over time. Because it had to.

He was also right that the road was isolated. They passed only a few old, barren-looking beach cottages along the drive that twisted between woods and swampy areas. Tall trees lined the road until ruddy asphalt gave way to well-packed gravel. "You sure it's not one of the places we already passed?" Jason Rose asked.

"My uncle said it was at the very end of the road," she replied.

And then suddenly the cottage stood before them, indeed squarely at the dead end of what had become a part gravel/part dirt path. Foliage around the house was overgrown, droopy and untended. The porch sagged. The place appeared as abandoned as her car was right now. "Oh," she heard herself breathe. This didn't seem like a step toward things getting better.

The truck came to a stop in a puff of yellowish dirt. "No wonder it's free," he murmured.

"My uncle warned me," she remembered out loud, trying to move past her disappointment. After all, it was just one more in a long line. It would be okay. "He said no one's stayed here in years. But he had the electricity turned on for me, and the water tank filled. And he pays someone to come by every few months and check on the place, make sure the plumbing's working and all is well. So it's probably not as bad as it looks."

"I'm sorry, but it looks pretty bad." He turned toward her. "I don't know if I can leave you here."

She blinked, taken aback. "Well, fortunately for me, it's not your choice." *And I have nowhere else to go.* She kept that part to herself, however.

He lowered his chin, gave her a frank look. "Honey, I'm not sure this place is even habitable."

And at this, Shelby pulled in her breath, her back going rigid. She knew he meant well, but the last thing she needed was some wannabe knight in shining armor. It was time to take charge of this situation. "First of all, I'm not your honey." She'd let that slide the first couple of times, but was done with it now. "And second—it's got four walls, a roof, electricity, and water, so it's *perfectly* habitable." Her standards for that were pretty low at this point. "And third, as much as I appreciate you stopping and giving me a ride, I'm capable of taking care of myself, and I don't let men I don't even know make decisions for me."

He raised his eyebrows in surprise, but appeared completely undaunted by her stern voice. "Well, maybe you should if you can't make better ones than this."

She gasped. "How dare you!"

"I dare because this is the twenty-first century and no one says 'how dare you' anymore. And you look like a sensible enough human being, but I'm not sure you're acting like one, so I'm being sensible *for* you."

Rather than reply, though, Shelby followed the very strong gut instinct to just open the door and get out. Because she didn't like even the implication of possibly ending up trapped inside, at someone else's will. Once out of the truck, she immediately rose on her tiptoes to start removing her stuff from the back.

The next thing she knew, Jason Rose was out of the truck, too, door slamming—still ranting. "And oh my God, woman, if you're really insane enough to stay here at this fallen-down shack in the middle of nowhere, I'm at least going to help you unload your stuff, so step aside."

"I will *not* step aside. I'm totally capable of—"

"Yeah, I heard you already and know you're capable. Capable of making silly decisions that put you at risk for no good reason."

That quieted her. But not for the reasons he probably thought. It was because she had *plenty* of good reasons—none of which she intended to tell him. She just wanted her stuff out of his truck and wanted him gone. They both continued to work at removing boxes and bags and clothes—in silence now—until it all sat heaped on the front porch.

"Well," he said, "let's get inside and check the place out. Do you have a key?"

He thought he was going in with her? Again, she knew he had honorable intentions—or she was pretty sure of that anyway—but still...nope. "The key is here, hidden," she told him.

"Because burglars are drawn to this place like flies," he said.

She shot him a look.

"So get the key."

"I can get inside myself."

"I'd rather help you."

"I'd rather you didn't."

He rolled his eyes, let out a sigh. As if she were the most difficult person on the earth. And maybe her need for privacy right now did seem a little weird, but he had no idea what she'd been through—or why she was here. "Why won't you accept my help?"

"Because—"

"Because you're a capable person who doesn't like being called honey—I know. But damn, woman—you make it hard to be a decent guy."

His frustration only escalated the tension, causing her heart to beat too hard. In another life, she'd have been happy to let him help her. But she just couldn't let anyone push her in that way right now. She'd been pushed that way before—too far. Into a box. Into locked rooms. Locked condos. There was no way to make him understand, so at the risk of seeming completely unreasonable and maybe even a little crazy, she said, "I want you to go."

"What are you going to eat?"

"I have food," she claimed.

"I don't believe you."

She blew out a breath. "I don't care. I want you to go."

Another disgruntled sigh from him. "What if you can't get the door unlocked or something? What if you walk in and it's worse than you expect?"

"I'll deal with it," she told him staunchly. It was almost a battle of wills now. "I just want you to go."

"You want me to go?" He sounded smug, sarcastic, disbelieving.

"Yes, I want you to go," she assured him.

He looked still more agitated now, his gorgeous blue eyes narrowed, his strong jaw set. "You *really* want me to go."

"More than I can say," she insisted.

He pressed his lips together tight into a thin, rigid line. "Fine. You want me to go, I'm gone."

And with that, he started toward the truck, tossing over his shoulder, "But don't come crying to me when you're starving to death. Or when some rat hiding in the floorboards bites you and gives you rabies. Or the ceiling falls in on your head." He rounded the front fender and reached the driver's side, peering at her over the hood. "Oh, and don't walk into the swamp—it's all around you."

He got inside, slammed the door, started the engine with a roar. She waited as he turned the truck around in the dry dirt in front of the house with jerky moves back and forth, and just when she thought he was finally leaving, the driver's side window—now facing her—lowered. "And watch out for gators," he said. "They're everywhere. Good luck to ya."

After which the big pickup rumbled away down the dirt-and-gravel path, leaving a trail of dust, until finally all she could hear was the sounds of birds and the occasional plop of something into nearby water, and knew she was finally alone.

Gators. She hadn't thought about gators.

CHAPTER TWO

The key, attached to an oval-shaped piece of plastic bearing the remains of a business logo that had long since worn away, wasn't actually well hidden at all. As her uncle had promised, it lay under an empty terra cotta flowerpot on the wide, bowing front porch.

The cottage had clearly once been white but was now more the pale gray of sun-beaten wood. Several once-green shutters were missing, one hanging at an angle from a front window. She spotted a bird's nest under the porch awning.

Her mother had grown up in this house, but Shelby had never been here before. As she turned the key in the old lock, she wished she'd seen the cottage in better days. But on the other hand, she was simply thankful it was here for her now. To Jason Rose, it might be a dilapidated shack, but to her it was a haven, a perfect retreat, the perfect place to start over.

The interior was predictably sparse, but blessedly solid-seeming—and at least marginally clean if you ignored the peeling wallpaper, some of which lay in curls along dusty baseboards missing much of their paint. The living room came with tall, wide windows that opened easily to admit a breeze that smelled like the sea. A saggy couch and scratched-up coffee table, both likely dating from the seventies, would be good enough for sitting, and for reading—since she had no TV. The kitchen sported a Formica countertop and non-matching Formica table along with a couple of old chairs covered in yellow vinyl. The faucet worked when she tried it, running water that, despite starting out brown, soon turned pleasantly clear as it ran down the drain of an old porcelain sink.

The cottage had two bedrooms, and one—as her uncle had told her—contained a bed. A white spindle headboard made her want to decorate the room in a whimsical sailing-themed blue and white—someday. For now, she was just glad to have brought a set of pale blue sheets and a white duvet.

The bathroom was simple and small, but the working faucets and flushing toilet were all she really required at the moment—though she made a mental note to invest in a new shower curtain to replace the old mildewed one currently curving around an antique clawfoot tub with a rusty drain.

One of the best things about the house: It came with an old washer and dryer that her uncle had assured her worked just fine. A tiny laundry cubby was situated near the back door, which opened onto a raised concrete porch that she envisioned perhaps someday soon being home to a small grill and a nice chair.

For monitoring the area for gators.

Though she shoved that thought out of her head as soon as it came. Her mother had lived here safely enough, after all. In fact, her mother had always *felt* safe here—she'd told Shelby that, more than once. Jason Rose had just been acting sarcastic by the time he'd brought up alligators.

All in all, the place was totally habitable. Especially when she factored in her lack of options. Sure, it was outdated, the floor sagged in spots, and the ceiling did, too. But as she'd hoped, the interior seemed in better shape than she'd feared it might from the outside.

Another point in its favor? It was so far off the beaten path that no one would ever think to look for her here. She'd never even mentioned to Craig that her mother grew up in South Carolina—thank goodness.

She went around opening windows, plentiful in a home with a near tropical climate. Thankful that the mattress looked clean, she put the new sheets on her new bed, slipping pillowcases on the two pillows she'd shoved in a shopping bag and brought along. She hung her clothes on the old rail in the small closet, below arranging the flip-flops and tennis shoes she'd packed. She put her underwear and other fold-ables in a small white dresser and bedside table, thankful for the practical pieces of furniture.

The sun had begun to set by the time she felt truly settled, so she plopped down on the couch, pulled out the cheap new prepaid smartphone she'd picked up at a Radio Shack in Kentucky, and dialed one of the very few numbers she'd keyed into it: her uncle's.

He picked up on the first ring.

"Uncle Gary," she said. "It's Shelby. I wanted to let you know I arrived at the cottage."

"And you got in okay? Everything is okay there?"

"Yes," she assured him. "Everything is just as you described."

"You see now I wasn't exaggerating about the shape it's in. I hope you're not too disappointed. Or uncomfortable."

"No," she assured him. "It's just what I'm wanting for right now, and I can add to it over time if I like." She'd claimed to her uncle that she'd taken a sabbatical from her advertising job and wanted to retreat someplace quiet for the winter to write a book. Not that she'd ever written a creative word in her life beyond ad copy or slogans, or had any such aspirations. But her uncle didn't know that and it had sounded believable enough.

"Well, like I said, you can stay as long as you like. And do anything to the place you want."

"Thanks—that's good to know." She wasn't sure what her future held long term, and at the moment, improvements sounded like a lofty goal—but at the same time, she sensed that the place had good bones and, if a person wanted to settle down here, a lot of potential.

"Ever since you called me, I've been thinking a lot about the old place," her uncle said. "Wondering why I never sold it. Sentimental, I guess. It was home to your mom and me until high school. And now that she's gone, seems even harder to think about letting it go—even if it just sits there unused." He released a self-deprecating chuckle at the lack of practicality in that. Shelby's mother had passed away after a short battle with lymphoma three years earlier, just after Shelby's twenty-fifth birthday.

"Well, it turns out to be convenient for me that you kept it," she said. More than convenient. The perfect escape.

"I'm glad it's getting some use. And really," he went on, "the place is half yours anyway."

"Oh," she said, a little stunned.

"I mean, sure, my family stayed in the cottage from time to time when the boys were young, and I've kept someone looking after it a little. But it was still always half your mom's—so now it's half yours. I think she'd be happy you're there."

Actually, she'd be horrified at what brought me here. Horrified that my life has devolved into this. But for the sake of her uncle she said, "I'm sure she would."

"Shelby dear," he said, suddenly sounding more serious, "are you okay on money?"

The question threw her. She'd thought he'd bought her

story completely. But maybe not. "Yes—fine," she said, though feared the reply sounded stiff.

"Okay. I don't mean to pry—I just wanted to make sure."

"That's nice of you, but no worries."

"I'm sorry we haven't been closer, with me down here in Tampa and you and your mom up north—but just like I told you after the funeral, if you need anything, I'm happy to help. And I mean that."

Her mind whirled with temptation—a few thousand dollars for a used car would be pretty handy right about now. But her uncle had a family of his own—including three sons, the eldest of which he was currently putting through MIT—and she had no intention of making *her* burdens *his* burdens. She was the one who'd gotten herself into this situation—she would be the one to get herself out. "I really appreciate knowing that—thank you."

"I'm sure it hasn't been easy on you, losing your mom the way you did, and being on your own." Shelby's dad had walked out of their lives when she was a baby, leaving her mom a single parent from a young age.

"Not, it hasn't," she told him honestly, "but…it's taught me to be resilient."

As they talked for a few more minutes, Shelby inquiring about her aunt and cousins, she got the overwhelming impression that hearing from her recently had left Uncle Gary concerned he should have been there for her more. What he had no way of knowing was that his having held on to the house all these years was actually the best possible avenue of giving her what she needed right now.

By the time they disconnected, darkness had fallen and she was hungry. Maybe she should have thought about that sooner, but she hadn't lied to Mr. Hot and Sexy about having food. One of her tote bags contained a few bottles of water, two granola bars, a box of Pop Tarts, and a bag of potato chips.

Carrying the granola bars and some water out to the back porch, she sat down on the edge and peered out over the darkening swamplands behind the cottage. It wasn't exactly a meal fit for a king, but she'd never enjoyed granola and water more than she did that night. Because gators notwithstanding, she was someplace safe, and that granola bar dinner had come with...freedom.

Of course, when she lay down in her new bed that night, windows open to let out the stuffiness that had been trapped inside, every sound became a mystery. Sleep didn't come easy.

Funny thing about freedom: Sometimes it also came with questions. *What am I doing? Was I crazy to come here? Was there some other way?* Not to mention that some of Jason Rose's concerns started to seem a little more relevant in the dark of night. *How am I going to survive here?*

But eventually exhaustion got the best of her and she soon awoke to the bright morning sun filling the uncovered windows, and the mere realization that she'd gotten the first night behind her brought back the sweet joy of liberation once more. It was a new day, a new beginning. There were problems to solve, but she would be just fine.

JASON ROSE WASN'T in the habit of drinking on his lunch hour. But that woman had driven him to it. Shelby. Shelby... who hadn't even told him her last name. And had, frankly, been pretty damn unappreciative, all things considered. Not that he was after gratitude—but she'd been downright rude to him just for looking out for her best interests. She'd come across as smart in some ways, but when it came to making decisions, not so much.

Of course, maybe he was being too hard on her. She'd been shaken up, after all. And clearly had more going on than she'd been willing to tell him. Even now, nearly a day later, she dominated his thoughts.

In his mind's eye, he still saw her long brown hair, pulled up in a messy ponytail, and the slender curves that had filled out her blue jeans. She'd possessed a cute smile—well, on the couple of occasions she'd been inclined to give it. Though her hazel eyes had teetered mostly between having a deer-in-headlights look and a tough, stubborn glare.

Despite himself, he was wondering how she'd managed overnight. If she really had something to eat. And what the hell her story was. He couldn't help worrying about her.

So after unloading a new shipment of Christmas trees at the nursery he'd taken over from his parents just last year, he'd told one of his employees, Tom, that he was headed to lunch. But today, that had turned out to be the Rose Tavern.

He pushed through the door to hear Springsteen belting out "Merry Christmas, Baby" to the sparse mid-day crowd. Rick had only started opening the place at noon since Jace had taken over the nursery, which had freed Rick from helping out there most days. Garland draped the long mahogany bar, and tiny ornaments hung from light fixtures, showing that his brother was doing up the holidays right.

As Jace parked himself on a stool, waiting for his brother to finish with a customer, he wondered how the hell he'd ended up here. He'd been the one who was going to leave, after all, get the hell out of Sassafras, have adventures. Yet in a family full of entrepreneurs, when his parents had chosen to retire last year, somehow taking over Rose's Nursery and Garden Center had ended up falling to him.

Although Rick had indeed helped with the nursery for

years, he had the bar to run, and it thrived in all seasons. His younger brother, Tanner, operated a successful construction business. So Mom and Dad had come to their middle son and asked him to sell his eighteen-wheeler to become a plant-and-tree guy. "You always took to it more than the other boys," his dad had said. "And you can't drive that truck forever."

Actually, he *could have* driven the truck forever—it was a job a man could do well into old age if he chose. But there'd been more to his parents' request than that. They'd always hated his trucking. They thought it was dangerous. They didn't like him being away for long stretches of time. His mother was certain "no woman will want to marry a man who's never home." As if he was looking for a wife. At thirty-four, he sure as hell wasn't—not yet anyway.

And while trucking was a job that came with a lot of red-tape frustrations, it had been lucrative and allowed him to see the country. He'd been keeping an eye out for someplace special he might want to move someday, as well as saving up a lot of money. Now, he still had his savings, but was no longer adding to it. And looked like Sassafras would be his permanent home.

Though the truth was, he liked the nursery work well enough—his dad was right; he was naturally skilled at it. And hell—maybe he never would have left for good anyway. But he supposed the thing he really missed most about life on the road was the sense of freedom and adventure it had given him. That little bit of excitement at not knowing what each day held or what lay around the next bend.

"Who peed in *your* Post Toasties?"

He looked up to see his brother approaching behind the bar. Their dad had asked that when they looked glum as kids, but Jace hadn't heard the saying in a long time. "Just wondering how the hell I ended up selling Christmas trees," he muttered.

"Middle-child syndrome," Rick said. "More important to you to please other people than yourself."

Jace rolled his eyes. Although he loved his brother, sometimes Rick could be a real know-it-all. And Jace thought Rick often erred on the side of pleasing *himself* first more than others, so could be he wasn't a fair authority on the topic.

He ordered a beer. "Give me a Blue Moon."

Rick raised his eyebrows. "Drinking your lunch? You must hate those trees worse than I thought."

Jace sighed and confessed, "Missing my rig is only a side irritation today."

As Rick poured the beer into a glass, then added the orange slice that enhanced this particular ale, he raised his gaze. "That so? What else is on your mind?"

Jace laughed. "When did you turn into a tell-me-your-troubles bartender?"

"I didn't. I'm a tell-me-your-troubles brother."

Cocking his head, Jace cast Rick a sideways glance. "It's a woman."

And Rick lowered his chin, clearly intrigued. "Tell me more."

"Well, wait. Not a woman like…a *woman* woman. Not a romantic thing or a sex thing." Jace knew he was seen around Sassafras as a ladies' man, so this story was going to be a big disappointment to his bro. "More like a damn stubborn thing."

With that, Jace proceeded to fill Rick in on the odd events of last evening. "You see somebody stranded on the side of the road, you stop to help—right? But you assume they're going to be a normal person, have some sense."

Rick shrugged. "Not really. A person on the side of the road is kind of a crapshoot."

"Well, she *looked* normal. *Acted* normal. Mostly. At first." Maybe that was the part he couldn't quite get over. Everything about her had reeked of being a smart, likable woman —until it had come to practically abandoning her car and insisting on staying in that ramshackle old house out in the swamp. "Maybe I should drive out there and check on her."

"Nah, I wouldn't," Rick said. "She made it clear she didn't want your help. And she sounds a little shady to me. Suspicious. Like somebody who's hiding."

"I'm more concerned she might be hungry than shady," Jace informed him.

His brother began wiping down the bar with a damp rag. "Since when are you such a good Samaritan?"

Jace had never seen himself as the hero type, never been drawn to a damsel in distress—but she'd stayed on his mind, too much. He knew, from his trucking days, what it was to be someplace new on your own. "Just seems like the decent thing to do."

"If you ask me," Rick concluded, "the chick sounds like trouble with a capital T. You don't need that. Leave her alone and let her be somebody else's problem."

As Jace drank his beer, he slowly decided Rick was probably right. You couldn't help somebody who didn't want to be helped, and she clearly *chose* to be left alone. If she was in some kind of trouble, hiding—which made unfortunate sense now that Rick had suggested it—he shouldn't get involved. Hell, she could be anyone. She could be some kind of criminal.

In fact, the more he thought about it, whatever her problem was, it was likely a pretty big one—and one she obviously didn't want to share. So be it.

Conversation shifted—what to get Mom and Dad for Christmas, if Tanner was still dating that Ashlynn girl from Edisto Beach, how Mia's painting was going. Rick's girlfriend, Mia, was a bona fide artist of the highest caliber and worked in a Charleston gallery, where she also sold her finished canvases. Rick said he'd drop by to pick up a tree from the nursery for Mia's Aunt Clara later this week, and also help Jace deliver one to their folks since Dad's back was giving him trouble lately.

Jace ate some bar peanuts to keep the beer from going to his head—and after leaving, he walked two doors down to Ida's Deli and had her whip him up a ham on rye. He called Tom—a young guy from a poor family who he was happy to give some work to—and said he'd be a little late getting back since he'd spent longer at the bar than intended.

He had Ida run him a Coke from the fountain to go, then got back in the pickup he'd pulled to a parking spot along the curb. Easing out onto Main Street, he spared one last thought for the ungrateful woman with hazel eyes, and pressed down on the gas. There were Christmas trees and pine wreathes and boughs of holly to sell.

Her life—her troubles—were none of his damn business.

So it was beyond his understanding when he suddenly made a U-turn in the middle of Main Street, knowing he was headed back out to Cypress Stump Road.

CHAPTER THREE

*A*s he turned onto the old swamp road, he realized he didn't have a plan. But he supposed he'd just knock on the door, likely get yelled at, but then at least be able to make sure she was okay. As okay as a woman with such poor decision-making skills could be anyway.

When he rounded a curve and a figure came into view walking toward town, it took him a minute to recognize her. Today her hair was down, falling in soft waves over her shoulders, and she wore a summery dress in a shade of orange that made him think of the sunset, with flip-flops on her feet. Shit. She looked...pretty.

Something about that caught him off-guard. Yeah, he'd taken in certain things about her yesterday, but today every-thing about her appeared...softer, more feminine, like the last sight you'd expect to see in such harsh surroundings.

He slowed the truck in time to stop beside her.

"Oh boy—you again?" she greeted him through the open window.

"Nice to see you, too."

"Well, I'm just wondering what you're doing back here."

She continued to walk as she talked—so he put the truck in reverse and eased backward at the same pace.

"I came to make sure you survived the night."

She spared him a glance. "Mission accomplished. So you're free to go."

And actually, she'd clearly done more than survive. She looked…like a woman completely in control of her fate, feminine but filled with purpose as she strode confidently up the lonely gravel road.

"Where ya headed?" he asked.

She looked straight ahead now as she walked. "To the market you pointed out to me."

"Delia's," he said. "Hop in—I'll give you a ride."

"Thanks, but I'm fine."

"It's a long way on foot."

"I like to walk."

"You picked the hottest part of the day for it, too. Get in."

"No."

"Why the hell not?" He'd pretty much expected this from her, but it still frustrated him more than he could easily understand.

She gave a smug shrug. "You're not even going in the right direction."

"Sarcasm," he remarked. "Nice."

Then he humored her by putting the truck back in Drive, making a three-point turn on the desolate road, then pulling back up alongside her. "Going the right way now. Get in."

Outside the truck, a huff from her. "I said no thanks."

Inside, one from him. "Well, I insist." But he was trying to keep his cool.

"No. Now go away please."

Trying, but he lost it a little. "Listen, woman, do I have to get out, throw you over my shoulder, and put you in this truck myself?"

And at this, she shrank back from him, frozen in place, looking threatened, and visibly trembling. This was more than a deer in headlights—closer to full-on panic—and a one-eighty from the stubborn, no-nonsense woman she'd been only a few seconds ago.

"Hey, I was only kidding." He tried to speak more softly. "Mostly. I mean—exaggerating. I'm just trying to do the right thing here, honey." Then he shut his eyes and clenched his teeth. "And I just called you honey again—because it's just what I do sometimes. But I don't mean anything by it. I don't mean…to offend you. If you're offended." He was officially at a loss, not even sure what to say anymore. Maybe he *should have* listened to Rick and not come out here. But his gut had told him otherwise.

"Perhaps the right thing is to just let me be," she told him. She'd resumed walking again, but her protest didn't sound quite as stalwart as before. It was the first time he'd heard her voice go just a little fragile. As if he'd uncovered a chink in her armor. But he didn't necessarily like having done it; hell, the last thing he'd meant to do was make her feel…weak in any way.

All he could do was keep following his gut. "Problem is," he told her, "that seems like the *wrong* thing. When I'm already here, in a vehicle, and it's getting hot out." Not summer hot—but the sun could still be strong here in winter, and today it was.

The woman outside the truck kept moving, though, putting one flip-flop in front of the other, the flouncy skirt of her sundress swaying with each step.

Until she stopped. Which surprised the hell out of him.

He braked the truck from easing forward as well.

And she pointed ahead at something in the distance. "What's that?"

He could just barely make out what she saw, a good fifty yards away. "Looks like a little gator."

Even outside the truck and a few feet away, he sensed her tensing up.

"Just out getting a little sun is all," he explained, trying to reassure her. "You don't bother him, he probably won't bother you."

Her gaze darted to his. "Probably?"

He shrugged. "I'm ninety-nine percent sure, but it's a wild animal, after all—so yeah, probably."

Next to the truck, she looked back to the small alligator—probably just a three- or four-footer—before glancing quickly at him and then down, letting out another huffing breath. "Damn it," she muttered. "Fine."

"Fine what?"

She hesitated to lift her gaze to his. "Fine. You win. I'll get in."

"Finally, she shows some sense! Hallelujah."

Not bothering to hide his victorious smile, he watched as she marched belligerently around the front of the truck, opened the door, and climbed up into the cab, that sunset-colored dress pooling around her. "But you're not driving me home," she warned.

"The hell I'm not," he countered.

Shelby was tired of arguing with this man. And she could scarcely believe she'd just accepted a ride from him after all the refusals she'd given. "Why are you so determined to drive me places against my will?"

He answered her question with another question. "How the hell are you going to carry a bunch of groceries that far?"

She despised the instinctive reaction that had snuck out in response to his comment about throwing her over his shoulder. Life with Craig had conditioned her in some negative ways. But even so, brave as she was and strong as she was, she wasn't ready to get to know the neighborhood alligators just yet. "I'll manage."

"This gator disagrees." They were driving slowly toward it, Jace easing the truck around its scaly, pointy tail. She cautiously leaned over to peer out his window at the prehistoric-looking creature as they passed, admittedly glad she wasn't on foot for this part of the journey and wondering if Jace had colluded with the gator.

"You realize this puts your offers of help one step above a reptile on my list," she pointed out.

He only shrugged. "I'm not trying to get in your good graces, honey." He flinched. "I mean Shelby. I'm just being a decent guy."

"Look," she began. Reasoning with him hadn't worked so far, but she'd try again. "I appreciate the chivalry—I really do. But I just like to do things on my own, take care of myself."

"Don't get me wrong—I can appreciate being independent. So happens I'm pretty damn independent myself. But you seem to be in a...well, let's call it a precarious situation."

"You know nothing *about* my situation," she snapped unthinkingly. She didn't even like the implication that anyone did.

"I know you're living too far from town to get around without a car," he shot right back at her. "Down a gator-lined road. Without any neighbors, and probably spotty cell reception at best. So I think I know enough."

Yes, she knew all that, too. She didn't need to be reminded. "It's not ideal, I admit."

A sardonic laugh left him.

She ignored it and went on. "But I'm taking things one day at a time here. First, I'm getting settled. Then I'll find a job. Then I'll get a car. It might not be...perfect—but I can make it work."

"I just don't know why you want to. I mean, when you have someone willing to lend you a hand. And a car."

Her gaze darted to the handsome man behind the steering wheel. "What?"

"I was thinking as I was driving out here—I have a spare car no one's using. Why don't you borrow it? Just until you get on your feet."

"No." It was tempting in a way because, like it or not, it *was* a long walk to the market or town—but there were so many reasons not to. She couldn't let herself owe a man *anything* right now. Even gratitude. She had nothing to give. And not much left to take. She had wounds to lick, and all that was easier if she was on her own, leading the solitary existence she'd planned when she'd decided to come here.

"Why the hell not?" he bellowed.

"It's...too big of a thing to borrow," she tried to explain.

"It's a piece of crap, actually, so not that big."

"I can't," she insisted. "I won't. That simple. It's nice of you —truly—but no."

Across the truck's cab, he let out a long, belabored sigh. "Why are you so damn stubborn, woman?"

"You actually seem *just* as stubborn. Just as determined to force your help on me as I am not to take it."

"Because I don't wanna feel like shit if something happens to you out here."

She shot him a glance. "Consider yourself absolved. There. Done."

Jace blew out another frustrated breath. There was clearly no reasoning with her. But to his way of thinking, that just added one more mystery to all the others already swirling around her pretty head. She wasn't dumb—he could tell just by talking to her. So she was making willfully risky decisions. What the hell made this woman behave this way?

He should probably take all the cues he was receiving—

from her, from his brother—and do what she'd just said, consider the matter done.

But something continued drawing him to her like a fly to molasses.

Up to now he'd thought it was just the whole being-a-decent-guy thing, the wondering-how-the-hell-she'd-survive thing. But he couldn't deny that there was something about her—underneath all that rigid stubbornness, she was cute. Clever. Again, pretty—he couldn't stop seeing that now. And yet at the same time undeniably tough for being in such a petite little five and a half foot frame.

She had amazing lips. So amazing that as they drove silently toward the market, he found himself wondering how he'd missed noticing them yesterday. Maybe too much going on—too much moving of boxes and bags, and confusion over not towing her car and her demanding to be left at that ramshackle old house. But now he was noticing.

Even as he stared at the narrow, pockmarked road before him, he stayed peripherally aware of lush heart-shaped lips the color of berries and wondered what it would be like to kiss them. He stayed aware of the waves in her hair, which separated into little corkscrew curls at the ends. He stayed aware of hazel eyes that mostly bordered between emotionless and angry, but every now and then softened, allowing him to see the girl inside the woman for a few brief nanoseconds before she covered it back up.

And he stayed aware of…that newly discovered but somehow downright searing femininity in her. Her dress, her flowing hair, her pouty lips, her freshly sunkissed cheeks…and whatever the hell had brought her here and had her living moment to moment hadn't been enough to keep her from painting her toenails a pale shade of pink.

As he pulled into the market's gravel lot, mostly empty right now, he said, "Delia's place is a lot smaller than the supermarket in town, but it's family operated, local, so I come here quite a bit. She'll be glad to have your business."

His passenger kept her eyes straight ahead. "And I'll be happy to give it. I'll…probably be here a lot."

"As often as you can stand to make the walk," he muttered, unable to help himself. He hoped she'd paid attention—realized just how long it was. Liking to walk was one thing—but having to walk a couple miles every time you needed *anything* sounded like a challenging way to live in this day and age when they'd all been raised to depend on modern conveniences.

He followed Shelby up the steps that led to the door, then held it open for her.

"Afternoon, Jace," Delia greeted him with a smile as they stepped inside. Bing Crosby sang "White Christmas" over hidden speakers. "Don't you have Christmas trees to be selling this time of day?"

When did my life get taken over by Christmas trees? He kept the negativity to himself, though, and instead said, "Tom's holding down the fort for me." Then motioned to the lady at his side. "This is my friend, Shelby. She's living out on Cypress Stump Road. Just moved in, so she's needing some groceries. You two'll probably be seeing a lot of each other."

"Welcome to Sassafras," Delia said, and Shelby smiled and said hello.

He hadn't seen enough of that, Shelby smiling. Her eyes sparkled. It tightened something in his chest. And his groin.

Damn, dude—don't go there. There's a great big world of willing women out there—this is the last one you need to be trying to bed. "I'll, uh…let you shop in peace," he said awkwardly, hoping like hell she couldn't see his out-of-the-blue reaction to a simple smile.

"That would be nice." She said it pleasantly, but with just a little bite—enough for *him* to hear it, but not Delia.

Delia's wasn't going to give her the choices of a bigger store, but it would allow her to go home with some staples. As she began perusing the aisles of the small market, he stepped closer to the proprietor—a no-nonsense forty-something woman whose parents had run the store before her—and spoke low. "Listen, do me a favor and, uh, don't ring up all her stuff."

"What?" She looked understandably confused.

Reaching in the back pocket of his worn blue jeans, he pulled out a wallet, and from it a few twenties, which he slid across the old wooden counter to her. "Just want to cover some groceries for her, that's all. Charge her enough that she won't notice, and maybe do the same until this runs out, okay? And when it does, let me know so I can add to it."

The woman's dark eyes rose to his briefly before she picked up the cash and slipped it into a pocket. "You're a good man, Jason Rose."

He sighed, shook his head. "I just think she's a little down on her luck and could use a hand."

"Well, she's lucky to have you as a friend."

At this, he just chuckled. Too bad Shelby didn't see it that way.

Fifteen minutes later, she wheeled one of the store's few pushcarts to the counter, unloading her goods. Jace caught sight of milk, soda, canned soup, bread, margarine, some fruit, cold cuts, cheese, hotdogs, a bag of potatoes, a box of cereal, and a few paper goods and cleaning supplies.

After ringing it all up, Delia said, "Twenty-seven ninety-eight."

Shelby stood up a little straighter, drawing back slightly. "Wow. Less than I expected."

Delia shrugged. "I try to price things competitively." Then she tossed him a quick glance—he suspected his first twenty had just gone to this particular bill and the next two would be factored in for future purchases. And when the receipt shot out of the cash register, she ripped it off, gave it a look, and said, "Low on ink—can't even read this thing. Sorry." Then stuffed it in the trash.

Shelby gave her head a lighthearted shake. "No worries."

The two women's eyes met and Delia motioned to the west of the store. "I live in a little house right over there. If you ever need anything—anything at all—and I'm not here, I'm probably at home."

Shelby smiled that pretty smile of hers again, and damn if it didn't have the exact same effect on Jace as before. "Thank you," she told the other woman—and he almost envied that she sounded a damn sight more grateful to Delia than she had to him so far.

Delia shrugged. "Women on their own gotta stick together. Never hurts to have a friend."

Shelby nodded, murmured, "Thanks again," then started collecting the plastic bags Jace and Delia had both loaded with her purchases. Jace rushed to grab up more than half of them before she could, though, along with the twelve-pack of soda.

As they walked back out to the truck, he wondered if she was realizing how hard it would be to get things like soda or a gallon of milk home without a vehicle, and he held out hope she'd decide to take the offer. For the moment, he was just glad she hadn't put up a fight about him driving her home after all.

"She seemed nice," Shelby said as they both got in the truck and shut their doors.

"Salt of the earth," he replied.

She nodded, and he could almost feel her weighing that, deciding if it was safe to like Delia, safe to consider her a friend. And he almost made a crack about her being nicer to Delia than to him, but then it suddenly struck him what the main difference was between him and Delia. He was a man.

And his mind shot back to the event on the road, where she'd drawn back when he'd made his smart ass remark about throwing her over his shoulder.

He glanced over at her again as he pulled from the gravel lot out onto the highway. *What have you been through, honey?*

As he turned onto Cypress Stump Road, he asked her, "House come with dishes? Pots and pans?"

She nodded. "Enough."

He'd never had to consider doing without anything that basic—what it would be like to start solely from scratch. *What's your story, Miss Shelby?*

"You got a last name?" he asked.

She tossed him a quick glance, still wearing a small smile. "No."

It made him laugh. "Crazy me for thinking you'd tell me such top secret information." Then he cocked his head in her direction to tease her. "You on the lam? A government spy? Witness protection?"

She sighed, but still looked pleased enough—which he suspected was about the groceries, that maybe she was relieved to have some food in her possession. "Just getting a fresh start, like I keep telling you."

And that was when he realized that...hell, any of the things he'd just suggested could actually be true. And come with reasons to be wary of men in the mix. And that it should all make *him* as wary of *her* as Rick had suggested.

And yet it didn't. Fly. Molasses.

"Listen," he said as they neared the dilapidated cottage at the end of the road, "sure you won't let me lend you that old car? Just an old Ford mid-size. Probably gonna put it in a demolition derby next summer. It's just sitting there rusting right now and I'd be glad if somebody got some use out of it."

When she didn't answer right away, he gave her a grin and said, "I wouldn't even care if you ran it into a ditch like the last one."

And at this, Shelby No-Last-Name actually laughed. And Jace couldn't deny it was the prettiest sound he'd heard in a while.

"Thank you for the offer," she said, gifting him with another of those rare smiles, "but really, no. I'm good."

And when he eased the truck to a stop not far from her front porch, he said, "Fine, but I'm going to help you carry in your groceries." And when she started to protest, he held up a hand. "Seriously. Stop. I'll put them on the counter and walk right back out the door—no funny business, I promise."

And then he did just that. Walked in behind her, bags and Coke in hand, lowered them to the old counter in the sparse room, then turned to go. He'd seen only the living room and kitchen, but was relieved to find them...not so bad. An old broom stood in one corner, showing that she was busy trying to make the place more comfortable.

Stopping at the front door, he realized she'd followed him back there. On impulse, he pulled out his wallet and extracted a bent-up business card—left over from his long haul days. *Rose Trucking.* "This is my number," he said. I know you won't use it, but I wish you would. Anytime you need a ride, more groceries, anything else."

She took the card, looked at it.

And then surprised him by actually making conversation, asking him a question. "I thought Delia said you sold Christmas trees or something."

"I do. The card's old, but the number's still good."

She tilted her head. "Big difference between trucking and trees."

He shrugged. "Big difference between Chicago and Sassafras."

"Fair enough," she whispered.

Jace walked out the door to the front porch, its once-white paint long faded. He should just go, call it a day here, consider it at least a minor success to know she wouldn't starve and to have made her smile once or twice.

But hell—one more time he followed his gut, turning back to face her through the old screen door. "Listen, honey —I mean Shelby." He stopped, gave his head a self-deprecating shake, then looked back at her. "I get the idea you've been...I don't know, hurt somehow, by something or somebody. And it's none of my business to pry into that. But if you need a friend, I'm happy to be one. If you want to hear the story of how I ended up a top-level tree salesman, give me a call. I'm not a bad guy. And I wouldn't really throw you over my shoulder. Unless you wanted me to." Then he winced. Hell, where had *that* come from? He was flirting with her. He was a world-class flirt—anyone in Sassafras would say so—but under all the particular circumstances with her, he almost felt embarrassed. "Sorry," he said. "That was weird of me. And I really meant everything I said about being a friend. If you decide you need one. Or even just want one."

He didn't wait for her to answer, which was good since she didn't. He just turned and walked down the few sagging wooden boards that served as steps and crossed the dusty ground toward his truck.

CHAPTER FOUR

$\mathcal{I}$t was funny how much the smallest things could mean. Never in her life would Shelby have dreamed that putting groceries away into old cabinets and an ancient refrigerator could make her so happy. But as she moved around the kitchen in the house where her mother had grown up, she found the task downright joyful. The old cottage wasn't exactly a palace, but her mother had been happy and safe here as a girl—and she knew she could be happy and safe here, too.

She wasn't used to planning meals on a budget, so she hoped she'd shopped sensibly—a skill she'd probably acquire more with a little practice. And though she had enough money to buy groceries and pay the electric bill for a while if she scrimped, it had come as a pleasant surprise when her order at the market had rung up so cheaply. She almost even wondered if Delia had made a mistake. But she'd tried to point it out, give the woman an opportunity to check, so now she saw it simply as fate smiling on her. Again, funny how much such a little thing—an order that cost less than expected—could mean, all depending upon where you found yourself in life.

Despite herself, she was thankful Jason Rose had come along when he had. Going forward, she'd have to buy less at one time. Maybe look for a cart or wagon she could pull. There was a shed behind the house she'd not yet investigated —Uncle Gary had told her the key hanging by the back door would open it—so maybe she'd find something inside useful for hauling groceries.

She'd been touched by Delia's kindness. Once upon a time, she'd been easily moved by common kindness from others, and had always tried to be kind herself. Now, when someone was nice to her, she bristled inside, unable to fully trust in it. Maybe she needed a friend here, needed to let her guard down, just a little, and maybe Delia could eventually be that person. But it was hard.

Somehow the idea of trusting Delia seemed easier—wiser —than trusting Jason Rose. Maybe he meant well. *Probably* he meant well. But he was too handsome for his own good. Downright hot, even. When she was around him, she suffered a gnawing awareness of everything about him. The way his dark hair curled around his ears and that he needed a trim. The way his blue jeans hugged his thighs, and the ample bulge in front. The way his large hands gripped the steering wheel, or grocery bags, or whatever else he happened to be holding on to.

Damn it, thinking of his hands made her heart beat faster. She supposed that meant she wanted them on *her*. But that couldn't happen, plain and simple. He might be the nicest guy on the planet for all she knew, but it would be a long time before she trusted herself to put faith in someone again.

And as for his thinking she'd been hurt, and offering to be there for her...she blew out another sigh. She just wasn't ready for that. She surely came off as some kind of paranoid nut, but she just didn't have the luxury of caring about that right now. Right now, her focus was on one thing—surviving on her own, getting a new start on her own, learning to live again…on her own.

After putting away the food, she used just enough data on her phone to look up a towing company—then made the necessary call to have her wrecked car brought here. She hated dipping into her meager funds for that, but didn't feel she had a choice. Maybe the fact that the groceries had been cheap would take a little of the sting out the bill when the car arrived in a couple of hours.

After that, she amassed the cleaning products she'd bought—and a few more she'd found under the kitchen sink —and tried to decide where to start. Last night she'd used an old broom from the laundry room to take down cobwebs and sweep the floors—next would come wiping things down with good old-fashioned soap and water.

As she stood by the kitchen faucet filling a bucket from the laundry room, she realized she was humming "White Christmas." She'd been surprised to hear it playing in the market—she kept forgetting it was Christmastime.

In her old world, Christmas came with sweaters and boots, mittens and hats. There was usually some snow by now—at least a little. The season usually brought invitations to parties, hot chocolate to drink, gifts to wrap, trees to decorate. How utterly different it would be this year. More of a non-Christmas. Just another day.

She turned off the squeaky faucet with a sigh. It didn't matter anyway, though—Christmas had ceased being truly joyful when her mom died. Before that, it had been a special time—her mother had always made it that way, and even into her adulthood they'd shared annual traditions she'd assumed would last for many years to come. But everything since then had just been going through the motions—and then, bit by bit, realizing that amidst her grief she'd let her whole life be methodically stolen away.

Though this was no time for fretting. In fact, it was closer to time for celebrating, even if that wasn't about the holiday. She had a roof over her head, food to eat, strong legs to carry her. That was worthy of celebration.

The rest of her day would be about cleaning and wrecked-car delivery—then tomorrow she'd investigate the tool shed. There wasn't much of a yard—as in grass—but plenty of overgrown greenery crawling up the house that could be cut down. Who knew, maybe eventually she'd have enough money to invest in a few flowers around the front porch. Or paint for the walls, or the exterior, or the kitchen cabinets. Or…well, it would take a million things to make this house a home, but this was at least a beginning.

"WHY DO you look so miserable? Get reindeer poop in your stocking?"

Jace looked up to see his younger brother, Tanner, flashing his signature grin as he shoved a cup of eggnog into Jace's hand.

Tanner winked. "It's the good stuff. Talked mom into letting me spike it."

They stood in their parents' living room for the annual tree-trimming party. For people who raised and sold trees, tree-trimming had always been a big deal.

"You need to put some lights in the ones by the road at the nursery, Jace," his mother kept telling him.

"The way we always did," his dad would add.

To which he would shoot them a look and say—as gently as possible, "If you want lights in the trees, you can come put them up yourself." He'd end with a smile, but inside, he was irked. They'd asked him to take over the business—he'd taken it over. Now they constantly wanted to tell him how to run the damn place.

But that wasn't what had Jace in a sour mood. "Eh, just not in the holiday spirit this year," he told Tanner. Then added a laugh to try to lighten his response. "Or maybe I've seen one Christmas tree too many."

Though even that wasn't the real truth. As much as he liked to grouse about getting stuck with the nursery, the only real issue was that his life just...lacked newness. Every day was the same.

And maybe that was why Shelby I-Won't-Tell-You-My-Last-Name had stayed on his mind. She'd taken a little of the same-old-same-old out of the last few days, even if unwittingly. She'd left him downright intrigued. And—hell—frustrated in more ways than one.

He'd woken up this morning with a hard-on and the memory of a dream about her. It was nonsensical, the way so many dreams were, but they'd been naked together, touching, laughing. Other than the dream, he'd only heard her laugh once. And he wanted to hear it some more. He wanted to make her as carefree and open as she'd been in his sleeping mind's fantasy.

Opening his eyes to the sun had been a disappointment. The dream had come with making her happy, taking away whatever made her so rigid and closed-off. He'd even tried to go back to sleep and recapture the dream, get more of what she'd been giving him—but then his alarm had gone off and another day at Rose's Nursery and Garden Center had beckoned. And even if he liked the work fine, compared to being naked with Shelby, it was a damn poor substitute.

Shit. His brother had been talking this whole time and somehow Jace had tuned him out. He wasn't usually like that, so he tried to tune back in. Apparently Ashlynn—who

Tanner *was* still dating—wanted him to go her niece's Christmas recital, but that was feeling a little too meet-the-family for him, and added up to him not being much into Christmas this year, either. "Yeah, I hear ya," Jace said, nodding convincingly, pulling off the notion that he'd absorbed every word.

Around them, holiday music played—Crystal Gayle, if he wasn't mistaken, was currently telling them to have a merry little Christmas—and glasses of eggnog from his mom's old-fashioned punch bowl clinked while ornaments were added to the eight-foot spruce he and Rick had delivered this afternoon. Relatives and a few neighbors made up the small crowd.

"Thanks to Mia," he heard his mother telling a neighbor lady, "I've been able to make the whole tree an angel tree." Indeed, his mom had always liked a themed tree—and Rick's girlfriend's art had made the angel tree possible. Specializing in angels—Michelangelo style—she'd put miniature prints of some of her canvases onto ornaments. Jace even had a rack of them for sale on the counter at the nursery right now and they were proving popular. His parents' tree had a variety of different angel ornaments, but at least a dozen featured Mia's art.

"Hey guys."

Both looked up to see the artist herself, eggnog in hand. "Your ornaments are a hit with the party crowd," Jace informed her.

She smiled. "So I'm hearing. You have no idea how happy that makes me."

He sort of did—he'd heard both from her and Rick how difficult it was to get a foothold in the art world, and he knew any kind of success helped, financially and otherwise. "They're going over well at the nursery, too. I'll have a tidy check for you at the end of the month."

Her eyes lit up. "Really? That's amazing!"

She was a nice girl and, in his opinion, Rick had actually been a nicer *guy* since she'd come to town—down on her luck. So Jace was glad he could give her good news. "Selling like hotcakes," he informed her.

Of course, that very thought put another down-on-her-luck female squarely back in his thoughts. Not that she'd ever really left them. Damn, what was it about her? The mystery? The fearlessness? The simple beauty?

Or all of that?

"Listen," Mia said. "I have a friend at work—Stacy—who saw a picture of you in my phone and thinks you're really cute." She gave her a head a playful tilt. "So I could show you a picture of *her* in return, and maybe we could double some night soon." She finished with raised eyebrows.

And normally Jace would be interested—Tanner and Rick both liked to say he'd never met a woman he didn't like—but something about his mood just now made him answer, "Aw, I don't know, Mia—pretty busy with work and the holidays."

She and Tanner both appeared equally stunned. "Really?" she asked. "You're not curious? Don't even want to see her picture? She's pretty."

And part of Jace was just as surprised as they were—especially when he heard himself say, "Interested in someone else right now is all."

Whoa. He was? Interested? In the mysterious girl Rick thought was sketchy and who wanted nothing to do with him anyway?

"Um, no offense, dude," Tanner said, "but since when does that stop you?"

Fair enough—Jace was well known for playing the field, not wanting to be tied down, getting antsy and often jumping ship whenever a woman tried to ease into exclusivity with him. His mother often worried out loud that he was the one who would never give her grandchildren because he wouldn't hold still long enough—that he was always on the move, whether that was over the road or with women.

He was as honest with Mia as he knew how to be. "Guess I'm just not in a dating mood right now." He shook his head. "Check back with me after the holidays if she's still into it then." Maybe his reluctance his would pass by then. Maybe little miss Shelby would be packed up and gone by then. Who knew? With someone surrounded by so much mystery, anything could happen.

No matter how she sliced it, the nights were the hardest part.

There had been a time in her life when that wasn't the case. A time when sleep felt…almost like sweet escape—from worries, from mourning after her mother's passing. But she'd felt safe then. And now…well, she was trying her damnedest to feel that way again, but when darkness fell each night, the rise of fear inside her told her she hadn't made it to safe quite yet.

She found herself staying up as late as possible. Reading. Cleaning. Thinking—about plans for the house, wishes for a time to come when everything would seem easier. She stayed up until she was so tired she ached for sleep. And most of the time that worked. Then soon enough sunlight would wake her like a breath of fresh air, telling her she'd made it through the darkness once more. Daylight just felt like a friend right now. In the daylight, she could see what was coming. Then she'd roll over, pull the covers over her head, and go back to sleep for a while, because a few measly hours just didn't cut it.

Sometimes she tossed and turned no matter how tired she was, though. Her mind spun, reminding her where she was, how she'd gotten here. Lying in bed in the dark in a strange place made it harder to tune out that part than when she was up, busy, doing something productive.

This was one of those nights. Every shadow on the wall looked ominous, every sound created worry. The weather had already turned cooler than when she'd arrived just a few days ago, so she'd closed the windows tonight—but the sounds still came in.

And no matter what she tried to think about, her mind went back to Craig. To moments when she'd first begun to see his dark side, when she'd first begun to understand exactly how trapped she'd become. All from trusting him in a time of weakness. A time when she'd so *needed* someone to trust, someone to love. Maybe she'd always worried there was something a little *off* about him—but she just hadn't wanted to see it, believe it. He'd seemed so perfect in so many ways.

She blew out a breath. Realized she was hot beneath the covers.

Perhaps she'd closed those windows too soon. So she pushed up from the bed and lifted the nearest one, grateful for the soft breeze she suspected came from the water, despite the woods between the house and ocean. She imagined it had helped keep her mother's family cool in the muggy South Carolina summers, and that it would do the same for her.

As she lay back down, Craig still loomed larger-than-life in her thoughts.

Stop. Think of anything else.

Jason Rose sprung to mind.

But no, not him. He's dangerous, too—just in a different way.

Dangerous how?

She searched inside herself for an answer to the question. Not just the don't-trust-anyone, don't-trust-another-man answers, but something that ran deeper. And she supposed it boiled down to the strength of her attraction to him. And to even how much stronger it could grow if she let it take hold. It was about not letting herself be taken advantage of again. Not letting herself be vulnerable again.

Nonetheless, when she was near him, something within her changed, percolated to life. And when he'd flirted with her, she'd realized—*oh boy, I could have this if I wanted to. Have him.*

And I can't. I have to rescue myself this time. It was the only way to true freedom, true peace of mind.

But that realization didn't take away the yearning in her breasts. Nor the pooling of desire between her thighs. It didn't take away visions of letting him touch her in those places, visions of him moving in her, filling her, making her come.

They were hardly restful, peaceful things to ponder. She lay there in the dark, covers off, body still hot and prone—knowing she was sweating from something that had nothing to do with the weather.

He stayed on her mind—a thing she wanted but couldn't have—until finally those thoughts took her into sleep, and then into sweet, hot, sexy dreams.

When the sun hit the window, she opened her eyes almost surprised to find herself alone. But then she came back to reality, and what her reality had to be. Another night survived, another daybreak reached.

Paydirt.

Shelby had just opened the old shed door to find a treasure trove of hopefully functional lawn and garden tools. Rakes, hedge trimmers, shovels, a ladder, a wheelbarrow, and even an old-fashioned two-wheeled lawn mower—the kind without an engine.

As she began chopping and cutting vines away from the house, she also began to wonder what she'd do with them— she didn't exactly want to arrange or pay for garbage pickup here, at least not yet—but decided maybe she'd Google how to start a compost heap.

As she worked, her eyes fell on a rusted old mailbox on a broken post at one edge of the property. She could even make out the remnants of her mother's maiden name— Webster—on the side, reminiscent of a time when people felt safe letting others know who they were and where they lived. For her, now, that definitely *wouldn't* feel safe—and even orchestrating mail service would make her nervous. So for now, the mailbox would stay out of use. She'd call Uncle Gary back soon and insist he allow her to send money for the electric bill, but otherwise, she couldn't think of any mail she needed to receive anyway.

Just like cleaning the inside, tidying up the outside filled her with a sense of possibility. It was easy to envision eventually having enough money to repair the broken gutters, rebuild the front porch, buy new shutters, and give the whole place a fresh coat of paint. Maybe take it from faded white-gray to a creamy yellow or a pale blue. Maybe there'd even come a time when she'd want to replace that rusty mailbox and have one of her own. She didn't want to be foolish, but making this old cottage look a little nicer injected an unanticipated hope in her heart. The time would come when the last few years would be long behind her and life would be better.

"And speaking of foolish..." she muttered to herself. Maybe she'd been foolish to pass up Jason Rose's offer of a car. It came to mind every time she suddenly remembered she couldn't just hop in her own and go buy a missing cleaning supply, or haul away her garbage, or start scouting about town for a job.

But three years ago she'd let a man who'd been just as handsome and seemed just as kind start helping her after her mom's death and the resulting funeral expenses.

Though she'd had a good job, her mother's illness and burial had been expensive, even with insurance. The moment she'd started dating Craig, he would rush to pay a bill she couldn't, or show up with groceries, or put gas in her car—always refusing to let her pay him back. It had seemed kind, from a place of affection, and she'd let it happen. And if she was honest with herself, it had been nice having someone take care of her during that difficult time—and she'd soon willingly begun turning certain aspects of her life over to him. She'd thought it was safe—safe to fall in love. Safe to believe in someone. And look where that had gotten her. Here.

So no matter how hot Jace was, no matter how generous he seemed—it wasn't prudent to accept gifts or loans or anything else from him that she hadn't already. A couple of rides was enough.

Even if, despite herself, she couldn't stop thinking about him. Even if she wondered what his story was. *Ugh—stop it!* She'd come here knowing she had to do this all on her own—why had the first person she'd run into have to be a drop-dead sexy man who wanted to help her? Double ugh.

That was when she yanked down a vine with a rake—to uncover white flowers, up against the foundation, that made her gasp. The shoots of green topped with delicate snowy blooms were by far the brightest, loveliest things she'd seen anywhere around the house so far.

The yard soon revealed other similar treasures. Bits of

wild-growing lantana on the edge of the property—perhaps leftover from an old flowerbed of thirty or forty years ago? And hanging from branches on oaks and other trees that surrounded the yard she noticed clumps of whitish berries and dark green leaves different than the foliage of the trees themselves. On the opposite edge, near where her crunched-up car now sat, she hacked down some weeds to discover a small tree sporting red fluffy, cylindrical flowers.

Red. And white. Perfect for Christmas.

And it occurred to her that even if this year it would be more of a non-Christmas, maybe decorating with what she had access to would make the house feel a little more cheerful. So she grabbed up a pair of old clippers from the shed and set to work on the project.

The white berry clumps were plentiful on one side of the yard, so she cut down half a dozen of the easier-to-reach ones with the idea of attaching ribbon or twine and hanging them in windows. The red fluffy cylinders and white blooms could go together in drinking glasses that would serve as vases—not exactly a poinsettia, but for her, for now, they would become Christmas flowers.

She pulled back a branch, ready to snip off the first red cylinder—when she looked down to see an old sun-grayed wooden sign that had been obscured by the wild foliage. Stepping back, she could just make out the remains of the word *Beach* in faded white paint, along with an arrow.

At first glance, it pointed straight into the marshy, swampy woods. But then she realized a path of sorts existed there. Overgrown, but it appeared to be on higher ground than that around it. And for the first time since arriving, she recalled her mother always saying they lived next to the beach, and Uncle Gary had alluded to that, too—but she'd forgotten about it until now. Odd, since that had been part of the appeal of coming here—but it had gotten lost in the mental shuffle.

Of course, as she peered up the long-forgotten and untended path, she heard Jason Rose's voice in her ear. *Watch out for gators. They're everywhere.* A heavy sigh left her.

Yet the beach called to her. More than warnings about alligators at the moment. She only hoped it wouldn't be one more possibly foolish decision as she began to pick her way onto the old path, taking careful steps, snipping away weeds and growth in her path.

She tried to keep an eye out for gators, but of course knew they blended in well here. And she thought about how desperation had really started messing with her powers of reasoning. With each step, her heart beat faster with uneasiness. *If something happens to you out here, no one will ever know. Triple ugh. But just keep walking.*

She tried to stay calm and move methodically without letting emotions in—both of which were pretty much what had gotten her to South Carolina in the first place. She didn't know how far she walked—probably not as far as it seemed. But eventually, she began to hear the gentle ripple of waves on the shore and soon enough she could see the way out— she spotted the ocean, its flat horizon far in the distance. Her heart beat faster from success, and anticipation.

She emerged onto a nearly flat stretch of brown, tightly packed sand strewn with bits of bark and dark seaweed. The ocean stretched serenely before her, the surf lapping softly at the shore. The very sight brought an unexpected sense of calm. And the fact that a glance in either direction revealed the beach was empty—no signs of life but her—made her joy complete.

Though a building with a multi-eaved style of roof common to the area—the wood the same sunwashed gray as her front porch—stood on stilts in the distance, at the point where the sand met the trees. She found herself beginning to walk toward it for no particular reason—curiosity perhaps. The few other houses on Cypress Swamp Road were set back in the trees and had looked as deserted as her own at a glance; she wondered if this place was empty as well.

But as she grew closer, she heard music—Elvis telling her that Santa Claus was back in town—and could see it was an open-air sort of place, a restaurant maybe. Up a handful of weather-beaten wooden steps, a large bar in the shape of a square rested in the middle of the structure, surrounded by stools, a few of them filled, with tables on the sides.

She stopped near a guidepost sporting arrows painted different colors. *Charleston* to the north, *Savannah* and *Key West* to the south, *Bermuda* to the east, and directly to the west, up the old wooden stairs before her: *Salty Pete's.*

Given her cottage's relative isolation, she couldn't have been more surprised to find a restaurant within walking distance. And a brand new idea had just begun to percolate in her head—when she suffered the unsettling sense that someone was watching her.

She glanced up the steps—and her heart skipped a beat. Jason Rose stood looking down, handsome and rugged as ever, his blue-as-the-ocean eyes pinning her in place.

CHAPTER FIVE

"You've got to be kidding me," she muttered. "Why can't I get away from you?"

He shot her a grin. "Just lucky, I guess."

She shook her head, still in disbelief. "Seriously—why are you everywhere I go?"

Standing next to the bar, he shrugged. "Maybe *you're* everywhere *I* go—ever think of that? I was here first, after all."

She blew out a breath. "What on earth are you even doing here?"

"Getting takeout. You?"

"I walked up the beach."

He looked confused, surprised. "And how'd you get to the beach?"

"A path from the house. It comes out maybe half a mile away."

He lowered his chin, his expression speculative. "Really? Had no idea."

She nodded. "I was kind of surprised, too. But then I

remembered my mom saying the house was near the beach. Nearer than I realized, turns out."

He tilted his head. "This path of yours—was it safe?"

Now it was she who shrugged. "Safe enough. A little over-grown, but on high ground."

"Better be careful you don't run into any—"

"Gators, I know. Yeah, I kept an eye out."

He pointed to her hand. "Gonna clip it to death if you run into one?"

She looked down to see she still carried a pair of shrub trimmers and winced at not having realized. "I was doing a little lawn work when I found the path," she explained.

He grinned. "I'd offer to help, but I'm pretty sure you'd clip *me* to death if I even tried."

Despite herself, she laughed. But quieted just as quickly—she didn't need Jason Rose thinking she was warming to him. Since she wasn't. Since she couldn't. Though she told him, "You're right, I would—so don't even think about it." Then she raised the clippers and scissored the blades back and forth in his direction, just to prove she meant business.

She climbed the steps then, looking around. A tall, lanky gray-haired man stood with his back to her as he dealt with a customer on the far side of the bar. Pushing buttons on a cash register, he bellowed, "That'll be nine seventy-five, Junior." The few people at the bar seemed to have empty glasses and at least one looked irritated. If there were any waitresses, they were well hidden at the moment.

"You gonna clip Pete for having his restaurant too close to your house?" Jace asked.

She shot him a sideways glance. "For your information, I was wondering if he needs any help."

"Could be," Jace said. "He's seemed grumpy as hell since I got here, and pretty sure he's down a waitress or two. One of them might have just had a baby, now that I think about it."

The news actually made her heart flutter. This could be perfect. Well, as perfect as she could ask for under the current circumstances. A job she could commute to without a car.

Maybe her unwanted knight in denim armor had the same thought because he cocked her a glance and said, "Don't suppose you've rethought that car offer?"

"No, and if you bring it up again..." She raised the trimmers once more, sawing the blades.

It made him smile. Which she felt deep in her solar plexus. *So stop joking around with him—at all. It'll only encourage him, and that's the last thing you need.*

He shook his head and murmured, "Have it your way."

"Crab cakes are up, Jace!" the man he'd called Pete announced then. He held up a white bag, the top rolled down.

"That's me," Jace said softly. Then looked her way. "You take care of yourself, Shelby."

She nodded. Didn't smile. No more fun and games. And as he circled the bar to the other side, she tried not to feel that stark awareness, that unbidden attraction he seemed to bring out in her more on each occasion they met. It was time to put Jason Rose out of her mind and get refocused on what was important here.

She watched from the same spot as he and Salty Pete chatted quietly across the way while Jace paid his bill—until finally she heard the older man grouse, "I can't stand around lollygagging with you all day, boy—don't you have Christmas trees to sell or something?"

Jace just laughed at that, and said, "You have a good day, too, Pete."

And despite herself, she fought down a vague sense of loss and disappointment when he disappeared out the other side of the open-air building.

Though there'd been a time when she felt that way whenever Craig left, too. *It means nothing.*

When the old man turned to face her, he struck her as salty indeed, striding toward her to gruffly ask, "What can I do for ya, missy?"

Remembering she still held hedge clippers, though her hand was thankfully lower than the bar, she set them smoothly on a stool beside her, out of sight, and said, "I need a job."

Pete pursed his lips, looking her up and down, his gaze openly critical. "You ever wait tables?"

"Yes," she lied.

"Work a cash register?"

"Yes." Another fib. Desperate times.

"Ever tend bar?"

"Only a little." As in never. "But I'm a fast learner."

He glanced around the place. "Slow in winter. Would only be part-time. Some lunch shifts. Eleven to three mostly."

She nodded. "That's fine." She tried not to sound too excited—even though she was.

"Can't pay ya much. Server wage plus tips."

"That's enough," she assured him. At the moment, it sounded like a Las Vegas jackpot.

He tipped his head back slightly and peered down his nose at her, clearly still sizing her up. Until finally he said, "Come by tomorrow at eleven."

She had to clamp her lips together to keep from squealing. "Absolutely," she said. "Thank you! Thank you so much!" Now she let out at least a smile, though—more elated to get a low-wage waitressing job than when she'd accepted her first junior advertising position in Indianapolis after graduating from Purdue. "I'll see you tomorrow morning," she promised, then turned to go.

"Hey!" Salty Pete exclaimed, stopping her in her tracks.

She looked back.

"What's your name?"

"Oh. Shelby," she rushed. "My name's Shelby."

Then he pointed over the bar, expression still dour. "Don't forget your weed clippers there, Shelby."

JACE PULLED in his driveway feeling pretty damn good. Well, bad in a way, too—because damned if that woman wasn't hard to figure, and maybe the most stubborn person he'd ever met. But seeing her had...well, it had made him happier than a few minutes with someone who didn't seem to want him around should have.

With her hair back up in a messy ponytail today, wisps of it falling onto her cheeks, wearing shorts and a yellow tank top with a smudge of dirt across the front, she'd still looked ridiculously pretty to him. What were the chances he'd get a hankering for some of Pete's crab cakes for the first time in a couple months at the exact moment Shelby No-Last-Name comes wandering in?

He was surprised to hear her house was situated so close to the thin crescent-shaped beach that rimmed that part of the coastline—but Cypress Stump Road had enough curves that it must dead-end closer than he'd realized. He wasn't surprised she was foolish enough to go traipsing off through the swamps—trail or not. He gave his head a slight shake as he slammed the truck door, takeout bag in hand.

Two dogs—a collie and a German shepherd—came running around the house to greet him. "Scarlett. Rhett. Settle down, you two." But he used his free hand to give them each an affectionate scratch behind the ear as he made his way up onto the porch and in the front door.

He'd been damn glad of the timing for more than just

getting to see her, too. It had given him a chance to put in a good word for her while paying his bill. Who knew—maybe it didn't matter—but that old coot didn't like most people on his *good* days and he'd seemed to be having a bad one. With any luck, Pete had just hired himself a new waitress.

SHELBY WALKED home from Salty Pete's the next day feeling on top of the world. Maybe for some people, this would be… well, nothing more than what it was: a low-paying job. But for her, it felt like the difference between life and death. It was food. Electricity. Clothing. Maybe eventually luxuries like a TV or a used car.

No, she wouldn't make much—certainly a pittance compared to her old paychecks—but she was viewing money through a whole new lens. She wouldn't need much here. The eighteen dollars she'd earned in tips today would go a lot further at Delia's market than it would in Chicago, that was for sure. And given that she didn't have to pay rent and had few other expenses, her new job would be enough to fund this new beginning of hers, at least for a little while.

She'd done well waiting tables—partly because it was slow, as Pete had warned her, but that had left time to study the menu, learn how the register worked, and for Pete to generally show her the ropes. She'd met the cook, a twenty-something guy named Reggie, who'd been cordial but seemed as into keeping to himself as she was. And before she'd left at three, she'd been introduced to Lonna—"Like Donna but with an L," the woman had told her—the evening shift waitress.

She learned in five minutes that Lonna was forty-two, had a teenage son and daughter who lived with her on the other side of Sassafras, and bunions that wouldn't quit. They needed to be surgically removed, "but who has the money for that, right? You gotta stay off your feet for weeks afterward, and I don't know about you, but I can't afford to be laid up like that. Gotta pay the bills, you know?" Being a talker, Lonna hadn't seemed to notice that Shelby shared nothing about herself other than that she was new in town, living nearby in a family cottage, and that she'd come from up north.

"For the winter," Lonna stated as if it were a confirmed fact. "I don't blame you. Who needs cold and snow when you can get away from it, right?"

Shelby hadn't corrected her, instead just nodding and telling her to have a nice evening as she headed out the back and took to the sand.

She couldn't stop smiling as she walked toward home.

Then it hit her, how she was thinking of the place. Less than a week and the stark little cottage was already becoming that to her. Very different than any other home she'd ever lived in, certainly, but the fact that it was hers, her private place to be, was a balm to any hardships she might be enduring.

That was one of the thoughts that often came to her at night when she couldn't sleep. That this was her private place. No one knew she was here. No one ever would. She was safe here and could rest easy.

Those were far more sensible things to think about than Jason Rose, that was for sure. She *whooshed* out a breath as a familiar wave of desire passed over her, along with a cool breeze blowing in off the Atlantic.

And yes, resting easy still came harder than she might like —but overall, the nights were getting better. Each night she slept a little longer. And she was beginning to learn the swamp sounds—mostly frogs and what she suspected was the sound an alligator made—and know they would bring her no harm.

As she located the end of the path through the woods, she decided tomorrow she'd find some way to mark it—something brightly colored to stick in the ground maybe—as it blended in and was challenging to spot from the beach. And maybe on her first day off she'd try to clear the path more, make it wider.

Despite the unusual tasks suddenly filling her life, however, as she made her way up the trail past thick foliage and Spanish moss dripping from tall, sprawling tree limbs, she couldn't help thinking that things were truly starting to fall into place—insomnia and adjustments to a whole new existence notwithstanding. She couldn't believe she already had a job. And incoming money. Which meant she wouldn't have to scrimp on groceries quite so much as she had these first few days. And also a home—that would be an ongoing project, but given that she planned to keep pretty much to herself, having a project was good. And not having much money would force her to be creative in new ways. Once she'd been creative about how to sell products to consumers. Now she'd be creative about how to recycle things, how to make something new out of something old.

And sure, okay—the money issue remained daunting no matter how you sliced it. Eighteen dollars did not a fortune make. But all of this was still better than being under someone else's control—and fearful for her very life.

She emerged from the path into the yard, thinking how much better things already looked than they had a mere couple of days ago. And that was when her eyes fell on something that hadn't been here when she'd left. A pale green bicycle leaned against the side of the house.

A heavy sigh left her. Jace. Clearly Jace.

Damn that man. He was so persistent, and so determined

to help her, whether she liked it or not. She wanted to slug him. And she also kind of wanted to hug him.

Approaching the bike, she discovered a large wire basket on front that would be good for toting groceries or other items. A small bell sat atop the handlebars. It was a cruiser—one speed—and lacked a kickstand.

She shouldn't accept it. It would set a bad precedent. She should just leave it exactly where it was and refuse to ride it. Or maybe she should find out where he lived or worked and leave it there—the same way he'd left it here. Though that might entail an awfully long walk home.

But…it was only a bicycle.

And if she was honest with herself, she was already starting to fall a little in love with it.

Yep, a new perspective changed the way you saw *everything*, even an old bike. She liked the color. She liked the handy basket. She liked that it felt old-fashioned and simple, just like her new life. And God knew it would make that new life easier. Delia's would be ten or fifteen minute commute. She could ride it up the beach to work, too, if she wanted—especially once she cleared the trail more.

So Jason Rose had given her a bike.

Just this once, rather than refuse his kindness, she would choose to be grateful for it instead.

But just this once.

CHAPTER SIX

good first day at work, brand new transportation, and a sunny, mild December afternoon made her decide to test out the bike and ride up to Delia's. But first she followed the inclination to pick one of the bigger white flowers from the edge of the yard—she thought it might be a camellia—and used an old piece of wire from the shed to attach it to the handlebar. Her mother had always said it was the little things in life that mattered, and she was beginning to understand that more and more.

No gators on the swamp road today, but if there had been a small one, the bike would have made her feel a lot braver about going past it. A little squeaky starting out, but otherwise it was easy and comfortable to ride, and she found herself smiling as she pedaled up Cypress Stump Road.

The market's parking lot was empty in late afternoon, making her even more relaxed in her surroundings.

"Shelby, right?" Delia asked when she walked in the door.

She smiled. "Yes—thanks for remembering."

"Well, any friend of Jace's..."

She was tempted to claim Jace wasn't her friend, but thought better of it, and just kept her smile in place.

"You getting settled in your new digs?"

Shelby nodded. "Slowly but surely."

"You need any help with anything, you let me know, okay?"

"That's sweet of you—thanks, and I will."

Delia just shrugged. "Like I said, ladies on our own gotta stick together."

She wondered if the other woman had caught on that she didn't have a vehicle and was low on cash. Either way, she appreciated her kindness.

She hadn't come to Delia's with any particular purchases in mind and was still fairly well stocked. But after noticing a cardboard giftwrap kiosk set up for the holiday season, she selected a roll of red ribbon. She could use it to hang the white berry clumps she planned to decorate with, and perhaps she'd tie some to a tree branch at the end of the path on the beach to mark her way. As she approached the register, she was struck dumb at the concept of a roll of ribbon being a splurge, a way to celebrate the earning of eighteen dollars no less—but she took a deep breath and pressed on. This was her new reality. And it wouldn't be this way forever.

"Can you tell me where I can buy a shower curtain?" she asked while checking out.

"They probably have a few at the dollar store just off Main, or maybe at the drug store across the street from it."

"Great—thanks!"

She asked Delia how far it was to the library, and got directions. There, she planned to use a computer to Google herself—most notably to see if anyone had reported her missing. She almost didn't want to know, but she *needed* to know. She could have looked on her phone, but wanted to save her data—and besides, it was nice to have an actual destination to ride to. If she was going to get more established here, she needed to learn her way around.

She still intended to keep to herself, but that came with limits. She wasn't trying to go entirely off the grid—just keep a low profile. And she'd found that dealing with people today at Salty Pete's and just now having an exchange with Delia was...nice. It made her feel human. Upon her arrival here, she actually *had* been planning to go off the grid as much as possible. But she was realizing now that she had to find the right balance in her new life. Much as she hated to admit it, maybe Jason Rose had started making her see it was okay to have a little human interaction.

Though it would be safer to do it with people other than with him. He was just too...everything. Sexy. Virile. Flirtatious. She wanted to engage with people, but without letting her guard down, and she feared Jason Rose had the seductive power to make her do just that if she wasn't careful.

The fact that she wasn't an experienced cyclist made her thankful traffic into town was light, and even after reaching downtown Sassafras, navigating on the bike was relatively easy, keeping to the side as a couple of vehicles passed her.

In Chicago, she would have needed to lock up a bicycle —*any* bicycle, even one without a kickstand—but as she propped hers against a signpost outside the dollar store, she figured bikes were likely a little safer in Sassafras, South Carolina.

Jackpot—the store had a selection of shower curtains. She bought a simple white plastic one, deciding that eventually she'd jazz it up by adding a more decorative cloth curtain for the exterior of the tub. For now, though, this would do the job.

After that, it was on to the library, where a friendly tree served as a bicycle stand. And soon enough, she found that no, she apparently hadn't been reported missing by Craig or anyone else. But given the way he'd treated her, and issues in his past that could make him look suspicious, maybe that made sense. And the sad truth was that probably only Craig realized she was gone anyway. She'd ended up so cut off from other people that it might take a while before anyone noticed she wasn't around. Nonetheless, it was a relief to be sure that even if Craig was looking for her, no one else would accidentally help him find her trail.

And who knew, maybe he wasn't looking at all. She'd felt terrified leaving, terrified he'd figure out some way to track her down. But maybe she'd misjudged him. Maybe it wasn't worth it to him. Maybe she'd gone far enough away, covertly enough, that he was truly in her past now—forever. That had been the plan, after all. And as she stared at the screen that brought up only the usual search results—a Facebook page she hadn't used in a while, other abandoned social media, her mother's obituary—she wondered if maybe that plan had actually worked.

Leaving the library, she felt downright happy. The crisp bite to the air told her the sweaters she'd brought south wouldn't go unused—and even a chilly ride back to the cottage as dusk approached would have her feeling hopeful about the future. Well, as hopeful as one could be with no address, an old bike as transportation, and a part-time waitressing job as her only means of survival. But all in all, things were better than they'd been yesterday, by a long shot.

Coasting back up Main Street, she caught sight of a familiar pickup truck—and spotted Jason Rose getting out of it.

The instincts that had brought her here, and stayed with her—self-preservation, wariness, distrust—told her to just pedal on by and pray by some odd stroke of luck that he wouldn't spot her. But all things considered, it made more sense to stop.

Even if just seeing him made her heart skitter. Made her begin to sweat despite the cooling December air. Made the crux of her thighs ache for everything strong and manly about him.

But just be cool. Casual. It's not flirting to stop. It's only being a normal human being.

She braked as she approached—only to realize that he was talking to someone, who was exiting the truck's passenger side against the curb where she couldn't see. He was even laughing—a rich, deep laugh that echoed up the street.

She wanted to keep going now—she hadn't planned on another person being involved in this conversation. But that was when he glanced up to see her and she knew it was too late. "Shelby," he greeted her.

"Hey," she said softly—just as a beautiful woman with honey-colored hair rounded the truck's hood.

CHAPTER SEVEN

*S*helby wanted to sink into the ground.

More realistically, she wanted to accelerate, pedal right on up the street as fast as she could. But she felt trapped.

"Mia, this is Shelby. Shelby, Mia."

"Hi," the beauty named Mia said. As friendly as Jace. Clearly having no idea Shelby was lusting for her man. They made a gorgeous couple.

"Hi," she managed in return, although it came out sounding too feeble for her liking. She felt like an idiot. She shouldn't. She'd had no way of knowing, after all, and he had flirted with her. But many a taken man flirted—it happened every day. She supposed she just felt like an idiot *inside*. To have misread him. To have thought the situation was different than it was.

"I'll be right in," Jace told Mia—and she cheerfully said okay, gave Shelby a wave, and disappeared into the Rose Tavern.

Shelby's heart beat too fast. From everything—seeing him, finding out he was with a woman, somehow feeling embarrassed, all of it. *But just try to act normal. You don't want anything with him anyway. You can't have that in your life right now and you know it.*

"Why do you look weird?" he asked her.

So much for normal. "Do I? I'm fine—everything's fine."

"That's my brother's girlfriend," he said. "I think I mentioned her to you. I gave her a ride to the bar since her car's in the shop."

And it was as if she could breathe again. As if a weight had been lifted off her chest. Like the world had resumed spinning after coming to a sudden, jolting halt. "Oh."

He grinned. "In case you were wondering."

"Not really." She shook her head, tried like hell to look uninterested, as if it didn't matter at all. "Seemed nice."

"She is." He continued to smile. Almost as if he knew what she'd been thinking and that it *did* matter. Even though it *couldn't* matter.

Get your head back in the game here. Quit feeling so relieved. Say what you stopped to say. "I wanted to thank you. For the bike."

He shrugged. "It's kind of a crappy bike," he said. "Doesn't even have a kickstand."

"I know. But *I* don't think it's crappy."

"Trust me, it is," he assured her. "I have a nicer one I don't use much, but I gave you the crappy one because I didn't want you to think it was too big of a thing to accept."

She'd asked for that, she supposed. "Well, I like it. And I appreciate it."

"I'm glad to see you out and about on it. And you added a flower." He pointed to the handlebars. "I like it. Suits you. Feminine."

And then their eyes met. And something inside her melted. It was as if he'd said more. Something about sex. The

68

chemistry between them was palpable, like some invisible force field wrapping around them.

"How's the house coming?"

"Fine, thanks." She wished her voice hadn't come out so breathless. She suffered the fleeting thought that she sounded like a woman who'd just *had* sex. *Good* sex. "And I got the car towed. And I got a job."

"That so? At Pete's place?"

She nodded. "Worked my first shift today."

"That's great," he said with a bigger smile than this particular job probably deserved.

"It's...a relief. To have a little money coming in. And a place I can get to without a car."

When he started saying, "You could have one if—" she held up a hand, quieting him.

"I'm good with the bike. I accepted it graciously. Let that be enough, okay?"

He laughed softly. "Okay." Then his eyes dropped to the ribbon in her basket. "Now, call me crazy," he said, pulling back to narrow his gaze on her, "but I wasn't expecting you to be doing a lot giftwrapping this holiday season. Do I have you pegged all wrong?"

A gentle laugh escaped her. "No. I bought it to hang a few...decorations."

He continued to eye her curiously, though. "Why do you sound so unsure about that?"

She couldn't help feeling sheepish. "Well, I don't actually *have* decorations. Just some berries and flowers I found. Red and white. So I thought it might make the place seem a little more Christmasy."

He just nodded, seeming to accept the reply and let it go, for which she was grateful. But then he motioned to the tavern at their right. "Want to come in? Let me buy a drink for a pretty lady?"

"Oh—no," she was quick to say. "But thanks."

He tilted his handsome head. "How did I know that would be your answer?"

She shrugged, tried for a small smile. "Guess I'm getting predictable."

"Predictable but mysterious," he declared. "Which is one hell of a weird combination." Then he looked back toward the bar. "Bummer for you about the drink, though—I get flirty after a beer or two."

"You're a *little* flirty with none at all."

He playfully raised his eyebrows. "So imagine how fun I am after a couple beers. You're missing out."

"My loss," she said. "Afraid you'll have to shower your affections on someone else."

"No one else I'm really interested in."

The words nearly made her heart stop. Jason Rose struck her a guy who was generally direct, but this took the cake. "Are you saying," she began cautiously, uncomfortably, "that you're interested...in me? That way?"

He tilted his head in the other direction. "Is that okay?"

She let out a breath. "No, actually, it's not. You can't be."

"Too late, honey—I mean Shelby."

Oh boy. She hadn't seen this coming. Yes, he had flirted with her a little. Yes, she was almost painfully attracted to him and her heart had sunk when she'd thought he was with someone. But none of *that* added up to *this*.

She chose her reply carefully, and gently forced out the words. "Jace, I thank you for being so kind to me, but I'm just not in a position to date anyone right now."

His eyebrows shot up. "Taken?"

She shook her head. "It's not that."

He took in the answer, processed it a few seconds, then cocked his head to one side. "All right. Then we'll just have to be friends with benefits." He ended with a wink.

And the heat that rushed to her cheeks told her she was blushing. Because she was envisioning them in bed together. Just as she did while trying to fall asleep at night. Such an alluring image. But that was all it could be. "Sorry. But I can't even really be friends with you." With other people maybe. But not him. There was too much temptation there. Too much raw heat.

"Can't even have a friend?" His eyebrows lifted—and then his expression grew more serious. "Shelby honey, I don't know what kind of trouble you're in, but eventually you'll need to trust somebody. I hope it'll be me."

She blew out a breath. And knew it was time to shut this down once and for all. "I have to go, Jace. Thanks again for the bike." And without another look into those gorgeous blue eyes of his, she lifted her feet from the asphalt and pedaled away as quickly as she could.

Jace sat at the bar, nursing a Blue Moon and wondering—for the millionth time—what the hell Shelby's deal was. Had she gotten panicky because he'd openly expressed his attraction to her? Or because he'd called her out on being in some kind of trouble? Maybe both.

Rick would tell him to keep his distance—which she generally made pretty damn easy if he didn't count this afternoon. Rick would say to let her take her problems with her and not make them his. But damn—she was hanging berries in a window in lieu of Christmas decorations? That just twisted up something in his chest, made him hurt for her in a way he could scarcely understand.

"Who's the girl?"

He looked up to see that Mia had just slid onto a stool beside him.

He considered his answer and finally said, "I'm not sure." Because he knew her name, but beyond that, not much else. Other than the mystery.

"Seemed like you knew her," she pointed out.

"Only a little. I gave her a ride when she wrecked her car. And I loaned her the bike she was riding." And like it or not, that pretty much summed up their relationship.

"She looked taken with you," she said. "Like all the girls."

At this, Jace just laughed. "Not so much, actually." And hell, maybe that was part of his fascination with her. Most women were openly into him. When one kept pushing him away, maybe it intrigued him.

But more than the intrigue, it was sadness that ate at him just now. He wasn't a guy who got all wrapped up in the holidays, but...hell, it would suck to be completely alone for them. Alone and...near destitute, as she appeared to be.

Since Christmas trees had become his life, Jace had stopped appreciating them much. But maybe it was one of those things that if he suddenly didn't have he would miss. So, sure, he still burned to know what had brought this girl to town, why she was doing without when she'd clearly had a better life elsewhere—but mostly, right now, he just wanted to do what he could to make it better.

She wouldn't like it, of course.

She'd claim it was too big, too much. Whatever the hell that even meant.

But he would just have to change her mind.

THE NEXT DAY, Shelby fell into the role of waitress with more ease—she was learning the menu better, getting used to how things worked at Pete's. At Pete's request—more of a surly command actually but she'd quickly grown accustomed to his demeanor—she stayed after her shift to let Lonna teach her a few bartending skills. The crowed stayed scant, as Pete had predicted, but she didn't mind—she still brought home twenty-two dollars in tips.

Day was already turning to dusk as she walked home up the beach. A more biting chill saturated the sea breeze, making her glad she'd brought a sweater today. But even beneath overcast skies blanketed with flat gray clouds, the commute felt peaceful—the beach in its stark but still beautiful serenity, the ocean in its vastness. Looking out on the unending plane of water gave her the impression of being on the very edge of the world, so very far away from Chicago, and that made her feel safe.

The walk up the wooded path felt a little more eerie, though, moss dripping like ghostly shrouds, and thick foliage jutting into her path, seeming like perfect hiding spots for alligators.

The night held the usual obstacles—darkness, isolation, and swamp sounds, which were becoming like white noise to her, but still held the unknown. The house was cool but not cold, and soon she'd need to turn on the furnace—and hope it worked.

Images of Jason Rose filled her head as she lay down to sleep. That seemed like a bad, bad habit to be forming. Fantasies of Jace…touching her, kissing her…ugh, it would just be too damn easy to misstep with him, let things happen. She had to hold on to her resolve.

The next morning before her shift at Salty Pete's, she got up early and fetched the hedge clippers and a hoe from the shed. Making her way to the path, she methodically worked to clear it. Despite being exhausted after a few hours of hard labor, she'd succeeded it making it much more open, wide enough to ride the bike through. She didn't mind the walk, but it got dark so early here this time of year that she welcomed the option.

After a quick shower in the old porcelain tub with her brand new shower curtain, she arrived at Pete's at eleven on the dot. An hour later, Pete pointed to a few white bags on the bar and said to her. "Delivery to Rose Tavern. Take my car."

She blinked her surprise. "I didn't know we delivered."

"We don't," Pete groused. "But that damn Rick Rose is always sending business my way when people want good southern seafood, so when the bastard asks for a favor, I feel obliged." He pointed a long, bony finger at her. "Shouldn't ever get obliged to people."

"I agree," she said. The old man was clearly trying to educate her to the ways of the world—without knowing this particular lesson was one she'd already learned the hard way.

She didn't particularly want to go to the Rose Tavern, but she tried to take the task in stride as she got behind the wheel of Pete's older-than-dirt Toyota. She just hoped Jace wasn't there. She liked seeing him, of course—far too much at this point—but she wasn't sure her heart, or other sensitive parts of her body, could take it.

And with or without his presence, despite her job at Pete's, she still didn't relish the idea of walking into an unknown establishment, putting herself in the middle of people. Silly perhaps, but Craig had filled her with paranoid fear and left her social skills pretty much in tatters.

Yet she was nothing if not brave, so after pulling to the curb, she slammed the door and carried the order in like a woman in full control of her existence. That was who she wanted to be, so for this moment, it was who she *would* be.

It was quiet inside—a few patrons at the far end of the bar, talking to the bartender. At a glance, she knew this was

Jace's brother—they possessed the same thick, dark hair, strong jawline, commanding stance.

That was when she glanced up—and became totally immersed in the amazing image on the ceiling. Jace had told her about the mural painted there. Cool he'd called it. But cool didn't begin to describe it. Breathtaking came closer.

Beautiful Renaissance-style angels that made her think of Botticelli and Michelangelo covered the entire expanse. Only these angels were...what? Sexual? Filled with longing? Lust? She was still trying to interpret the grand, enveloping sight above her when someone said, "Hi."

She drew her gaze down to find the artist herself, the woman she'd met with Jace.

"Hey, aren't you Jace's friend? Shelby, was it?"

She nodded. "Yes—hi. Nice to see you again."

Mia—Jace had said her name was Mia. And it was so much easier to like her now that she knew there was nothing romantic or sexual between her and Jace. The man she kept trying to avoid. However much sense that made. But this whole period of her life bordered on surreal, so she wasn't going to beat herself up for not succumbing to desires that felt dangerous.

Shelby held up her bags. "Delivery from Salty Pete's."

Mia raised her eyebrows. "You're working for Pete? Small world."

"Isn't it, though." In Sassafras, especially. Though Shelby was banking on it actually being a very, very big world beyond this little coastal town. A world so big that she'd never be found. At least until a time came when it felt a little safer to be more visible. But one day at a time.

To avert any questions about herself, she pointed to the ceiling. "Jace told me you painted this. It's incredible."

Mia's eyes lit up at the compliment. "Thank you!" She glanced at Rick Rose behind the bar, still in conversation with customers. "Not everyone gets it—not even him, and I'm lucky he didn't paint over it." She grinned. "It might be a little out there for Sassafras. So it always makes my day to hear a kind word about it."

Shelby leaned her head back to study it some more. "I love it. It makes me want to...lie on the bar and look at it for hours." Given that the mural covered the whole ceiling, she sensed it would *take* hours to truly soak in every artistic detail. "Though...am I right that they're, like, reaching for each other? Like in a passionate, romantic way?" She squinted slightly, unsure she had that part right. And hoped it wasn't a weird thing to ask.

But Mia nodded. "Exactly. They're reaching for each other, but they can't ever fulfill those desires."

Oh, sort of like I feel, about Jace. She instantly related to those angels far too well.

"Because they're not human," Mia went on, "and only humans can experience that. It's about the angels sort of... being in awe of us, wishing they could know the passion we do."

A slight gasp left Shelby at the words. "That's an amazing concept."

As the women talked more, she learned a bit about the gallery where Mia worked, and that she was off for the holidays and helping Rick with the bar until the new year.

The conversation made something in Shelby perk to life. Talk of culture, art, made her feel as if she were...someplace familiar, even though she wasn't. It was simply nice to be in the presence of someone she might have things in common with. If she didn't need to keep to herself, she thought she and Mia might be friends.

But as it was, they would remain acquaintances.

The angels stayed on her mind, though, even after leaving, and she spent the drive back to Pete's hoping she wouldn't be like Mia's angels—eternally trapped in a state of longing for something she couldn't have.

The afternoon at the restaurant was quieter than the previous ones—and she rode the bike back up the beach with only fifteen dollars in her pocket, but it still felt like a day well spent. And payday would come soon.

She thought about finances as she turned the bike up the newly cleared path—so much friendlier and less ominous-feeling now. She'd never had to live paycheck to paycheck before—or with such *small* paychecks—but she'd make it, and soon enough be able to take steps toward a better job and a more stable existence. Despite another day of overcast winter skies in low country, life continued looking brighter every day.

She emerged from the path into the barren yard, happy to see her little cottage, ready for a restful evening. Maybe she'd make soup and grilled cheese. Maybe she'd start reading a new book. Maybe she'd turn in early—and hope that sleep found her more quickly than usual these days.

That was when she pedaled around to the front of the house—to see Jace's truck, and to find the man himself standing on her front porch holding up a six-foot-tall pine tree.

CHAPTER EIGHT

She blinked her dismay and irritation. "Don't you have Christmas trees to sell?"

He answered with one of his full-bodied laughs. "Why does everybody keep asking me that?"

"Well, you claim to sell Christmas trees, but you never seem to be doing it—you always seem to be where *I* am."

He shifted his weight from one workboot to the other. "Truth is, they mostly sell themselves—and I have a couple of guys who can handle things just fine when I'm away."

She rolled her eyes. "Sounds like you lead a charmed life."

"Wouldn't go that far," he countered, "but I can make a personal delivery when I want to."

She took a deep breath, blew it back out. "So that's a Christmas tree," she said, looking to the pine he held upright on her porch.

"Well, not yet, technically. But once we get some lights and decorations on it…"

"I don't *have* lights and decorations."

He pointed to two cardboard boxes she hadn't yet noticed sitting on the porch. "Yes you do. I came prepared."

Shelby stopped a moment, caught her breath, tried to think through this. It was a very kind gesture. But no matter how she approached it, it seemed like a terrible idea. "Look, Jace—I know you're trying to be nice here, and I appreciate the trouble you've gone to. I really do. But I can't accept it."

He didn't look the least bit surprised by her response—or the least bit daunted. Apparently he'd gotten used to this. He simply tilted his head to one side, flashing a sexy little grin. "So after I lugged this stuff all the way out here, you'd make me put it back in the truck and take it away?"

"It's too much," she told him.

He gave her a pointed look. "It's a Christmas tree. From a guy who has about two hundred of them at the moment. It's really a pretty *small* thing. Next to nothing. Christmas is coming fast—I won't sell everything I have at this point, and there's a good chance this tree would go to waste anyway. So do you want this poor tree to have been cut down for nothing, or do you want to let it live out its purpose?"

She released a sigh. "I really doubt the tree cares at this point."

"But I do. My mother raised me not to let things go to waste."

She tipped her head back, out of arguments, and now it was she who shifted from one foot to the other. "You're impossible, you know that?"

He shrugged. "Been called worse. Now open up this door so I can get this thing situated."

Against her better judgment, Shelby climbed the few worn steps and let him inside. And of course he'd brought a watering stand for it, too—he'd left nothing unthought of.

"Don't act like it's such a big thing," he told her regarding the stand when she commented. "I run a nursery and was raised there. I know how to take care of a tree, cut or in soil. No big thing. Now where do you want it?"

The room sat mostly empty, leaving plenty of spots. "Maybe near the hearth?" She pointed. "It might be nice if I wanted to start a fire." It had just hit her that it could also provide cheaper heat than the furnace—she'd just have to come up with some firewood.

"Well, not until I can get a look in that chimney and clean it out," he told her.

Crap, he was right. "You don't have to," she was quick to say.

"Of course I don't. But I want to."

"You can't," she insisted, holding her hands up in a stopping motion.

That was when he turned to her, gripping her wrists in both his fists. "Stop," he said, soft but firm. "I want to. And it's a safety issue. So I'll look at it this weekend." It put their faces close, so close that her heart beat faster. Not in any sort of fear—but like the angels on the ceiling at the bar. If angels had physical hearts.

He dropped her wrists, took a step back—and she missed the touch instantly. He looked uncomfortable, and she knew he'd felt it, too—desire. And unlike with the angels, this desire could be fulfilled—but she supposed he knew better. Knew she'd push him away. Thank God he'd made that decision for her.

"Why are you so damn bad at accepting a little help?" he asked, now awkwardly moving the tree in its stand over near the small hearth.

"It's a long story," she murmured.

He glanced up from where he crouched by the stand. "I'm a good listener."

But she shook her head. "Let's just decorate the tree."

And to her surprise, this brought a smile to his face. "Now you're talkin', girl." And she realized that, in fact, he'd gotten her to agree to exactly what he'd originally come here for.

And perhaps that should make her feel manipulated. But mostly, she felt as if she'd dodged a bullet when he'd let her "long story" go so easily.

Just decorate the tree. Decorate the tree and...keep being careful with him. Don't let this go any further. Even if your heart tells you he's a good guy, a really good guy. Better to just keep things simple here.

As they dug into the boxes he'd brought, she found a strand of lights, but was informed by Jace that they'd be improvising on some of the decorations. She glanced over at him. "Improvising how?"

He reached in a grocery bag he'd also carried in and pulled out a packet of popcorn. "We'll be stringing this after we pop it," he explained. "Got needles and thread from my mom when I stopped by her place for a few spare ornaments, and some cinnamon sticks to add to the strings, too."

She blinked. "I've never strung popcorn before."

He gave his head a teasing shake. "City girl."

"You've done this a lot then?"

"Only all my damn life. Whether I wanted to or not."

She laughed. "Forced popcorn stringing? Sounds like a rough upbringing."

He let out a laugh, then informed her, "My mother's big into Christmas. Little bit of a slavedriver about it." Then he tossed her a look. "She was glowing with pride when I stopped by her place for supplies."

She released an acceptant sigh. "Well, I'm glad my holiday need resulted in something positive for someone."

The grin he gave her in reply echoed through her soul. She was feeling his presence too much. But there wasn't much she could do about it—at least not until they got this tree finished. And sounded like it might take a while.

Even more so when he added, "She gave me some ornaments, but not enough. So…" He took the lid off another box —to reveal a pile of pinecones and nuts inside.

"What the hell…?" she whispered.

It made him chuckle once more. "I'm guessing the city girl never made ornaments by hand, either."

"No," she said softly.

"Whether I like it or not, if there's one thing growing up as my mother's son taught me, it's that pretty much anything can look decent on a tree with a little paint and ribbon added to it."

SHELBY NEVER WOULD HAVE BELIEVED a man could look so masculine using white ribbon and a glue gun to transform a pinecone and an acorn into an angel. She was supposed to be making them, too, but repeatedly found herself caught up in watching the way he used his hands to turn such simple items into something worthy of hanging on a Christmas tree.

They made pinecone angels and a few pinecone reindeer, as well, adding twigs for antlers and legs. On the angels, the ribbon became wings. The scents of pine and cinnamon filled the little house, making it truly start to feel like Christmas to Shelby for the first time.

The strangest Christmas of her life, but at least now there were…markers. Of the season. And who knew—maybe later it would depress her. Maybe she'd decide it was easier not to miss Christmases past if she didn't have to be reminded of Christmas present—but for right now anyway, the scents soothed something inside her when being soothed was the last thing she'd expected.

They popped the popcorn in a skillet, the old-fashioned way, since the house didn't have a microwave—another item on her mental list for the future.

After stringing popcorn—which she learned from Jace took a soft touch, and which made her think of other more scintillating kinds of soft touches he might deliver—she realized it was nearly eight o'clock and she was hungry. She offered to make grilled cheese and heat up some canned soup, but Jace surprised her yet again, saying, "Almost forgot. Mom insisted on sending me with sandwiches. Hope you like egg salad." He winked.

"I do," she said softly. She lifted her gaze to his over their supplies spread messily on the kitchen table. "Homemade, I suppose?"

"She wouldn't have it any other way," he told her.

She got out sodas and some pretzels, along with two old Melmac plates from a cabinet, which she suspected her mother and grandparents had eaten from once upon a time. "And who does your mom think she made this sandwich for who is so in need of Christmas decorations?"

He flicked his gaze from his sandwich to her. "A friend."

"That's all?" She raised her eyebrows. "You tell her 'a friend' and she doesn't want to know more? My mother would have wanted to know more."

He laughed. "Of course she wants to know more. But she also knows prying won't get her anywhere with her boys so she doesn't even try."

When they'd both cleared their plates a few minutes later, Jace smiled at her and said, "Ready to trim this tree?"

"Yes—finally!" she said on a laugh. "I was starting to think we'd never actually get to this part."

Together they draped the edible garland over the lights Jace had already arranged on the boughs of the tree—a spruce, he'd informed her. Then they began hanging the ornaments they'd created, having used ribbon to shape hangers.

And it surprised her to discover Jace was right—simple as

it was, the tree was lovely. She wished her mother could have seen it sitting in her girlhood living room, making the place feel more like a home than Shelby could have imagined a week ago.

"Got a few more," Jace told her then, digging in a bag to draw out pieces of rolled up tissue paper. Unfurling them, he revealed half a dozen ceramic ornaments. And these, she saw, leaning near, featured Mia's angels.

"The angels from the tavern!" she said. She'd mentioned to him that she'd delivered lunch there today.

"I've been selling these for Mia at the nursery."

"Can I pay you for them?" she asked. Not that she could afford to spend money on something so frivolous, but it seemed the right thing to do and the ornaments were true works of art.

"No, Shelby honey, these are on me," he said. "Consider it my way of supporting an up-and-coming artist."

"And helping out *a friend* at the same time," she reminded him, putting air quotes around the key words.

"Ah, so I've officially advanced to friend," he said. "After you told me we couldn't be. Friends."

She hardly knew how to reply. She wanted to be so much more than friends with Jason Rose. It pulsed through every pore of her body the longer she was around him. But finally she settled on, "I guess you talked me into it."

"A good first step," he said, hanging one of the ceramic angel ornaments.

"First step," she repeated, confused. "Toward what?"

He kept his eyes on what he was doing—until finally tossing her a devilish glance. "Benefits? Or more?"

His playful manner drew an embarrassed and unwitting smile from her, her cheeks flushing with heat despite the house being comfortably cool. Yet she found her wits enough to say, "Afraid you can't buy me with a Christmas tree, Mr. Rose."

He leaned near enough that she drank in the male scent of him—pine and musk and a hint of something she couldn't identify. "Can't blame a guy for trying to make a move on a pretty girl, Miss..."

She met his gaze with a brief sideways glance, then looked away, not answering. Being coy. Not on purpose. An instinctive response. A mating dance she hadn't meant to perform, but it had just happened.

He didn't press further—but instead simply stood back and admired their work. "Well, if you ask me, it looks pretty damn nice."

She couldn't deny it. "It does." She let out another smile. "It really does. Thank you, Jace."

"Thank *you*—for accepting it." Then he held up a finger. "Almost forgot, one more thing." He pointed over his shoulder. "In the truck."

And with that he was out the door into the darkness, leaving her to realize he'd completely transformed the room. Before, the entirety of her Christmas had been white berries hanging in windows and on the front porch, and a few flowers on the mantle. This was immeasurably better. Closer to what a new beginning should look like.

A moment later, he came back in toting a large pine wreath decorated with thick red grosgrain ribbon.

Before she could say a word, he held up his other hand, producing the necessary hanging tools. "Even got a hammer and nail to put this thing over the mantle."

"You do think of everything." She just shook her head. Then watched as Jace hung the wreath above the fireplace.

They both agreed that it created the perfect finishing touch. The room, while still in need of many things, looked way less sparse and far warmer than before Jace had arrived.

And she already knew she'd miss the tree after the holidays when it was gone.

"Well," she began, "this has been...so, so nice of you. And I really love the tree."

"But it's time for me to go," he finished for her, a small grin on his handsome face.

"Yeah," she whispered.

And together they walked to the door. She held it open as he stepped outside, then followed him out onto the covered porch.

"Thank you again," she said. "And please thank your mother for me. But of course, don't tell her who I am since I'm not really interested in socializing."

A short guffaw left him. "You mystify me," he said.

But she shook her head. "I'm more simple than mysterious underneath it all—promise."

His eyes flitted over her head, then back down to her face. Heat filled his gaze—a heat she felt inside and that expanded outward through her chest. "I don't buy it," he informed her.

Their looks met and held—she felt locked in place, held tight by the same magnetic desire that had been growing between them all this time and had pulsated between them through the evening. Oh Lord, it was definitely time to end this. "Goodnight," she said.

He answered by lifting his hands to her face and bending to kiss her.

As his mouth met hers, pleasure shot through her like a rocket—but shock gave her the strength to press her palms to his chest and shove him a step back. "What was *that*?"

His eyes went wide, defensive. "You were standing under the mistletoe—what was I *supposed* to do?"

She blinked, confused, stunned. "Mistletoe?" Then she looked over her head—and saw a clump of the white berries she'd been using as decorations. "*That's* mistletoe?"

A hardy laugh left him. "Yes—you didn't know that? It's all over your house—I thought you were just *dying* for me to kiss you." He ended with a wink that nearly turned her inside out.

"No," she emphatically informed him. "I had no idea."

"But you were still dying for me to kiss you."

She blew out a breath. Direct as hell, this guy. So she'd have to be direct back. "Maybe. But I can't." She shook her head. "I really just can't."

"Why not?" His tone said he felt entitled to know at this point and she almost couldn't blame him.

"Lots of reasons," she whispered, shaking her head some more. "It's complicated."

"Do you want to tell me?" he asked.

"No." Yet another head shake.

"Do you want to kiss me?"

God, was it as easy as he was making it sound? A simple choice—do what feels best in the moment? Hedonistic thinking seemed like a road to ruin here, especially at a time in her life when caution was key.

And yet, despite her best intentions, the answer left her unbidden. "Yes."

CHAPTER NINE

It was official, Jason Rose had finally worn her down, finally pressed through all her defenses. She'd been so resolute, so determined. She'd put up strong walls, comprised of logic, fear, and a will to survive. And yet, barely more than a week after reaching the Carolina coast, she was letting a man kiss her. Letting those kisses melt down into her, consume her.

Her knees literally weakened as Jace eased his tongue between her lips to mingle with hers. It sent licks of fire shooting down through her breasts and between her thighs. She couldn't quite touch him back in the ways he was touching her—due to some small ounce of reserve still left inside her—but as he cupped her face back in his hands, she let hers curl into uneasy fists, let herself lean into his chest.

Even that tentative touch, though, brought her closer to his very maleness. His chest stretched broad and firm beneath her hands. His mouth was warm on hers, each kiss making her forget her reasons for caution a little more. She kissed him back not out of choice, but from pure animal instinct—her responses were almost beyond her control. It had been that way with him all along—and now she'd finally surrendered.

She almost hated this side of herself in this moment. She knew women were supposed to love and embrace their sexuality—but succumbing to it just now felt like a weakness, a trap. Craig had made it that way for her. And he'd made her hate sex. She'd thought living without it would be easy, that she wouldn't ever want it again, or at least not for a long time —but damn if meeting Jason Rose hadn't changed all that in a heartbeat.

And even so, that certain degree of timidity remained. So much that between kisses she heard herself softly confess near his ear, "I'm nervous."

"Why?" he whispered back.

She gave her usual answer in one word. "Complicated."

He drew back just enough to peer into her eyes on the dark porch, lit only by lamplight from inside. "I can be gentle."

"Please," she breathed.

It seemed a foregone conclusion that this wouldn't stop at just kissing. Even though she knew it ought to, knew she should find it in herself to end it right now.

That thought vanished, of course, when he resumed the kisses. Deep and passionate, yet at the same time she could sense him holding back, trying to do what he'd said, be gentle. *What is it like when you're* not *gentle?* She stopped the thought as quickly as it came, though—gentle was exactly what she needed right now.

He stopped kissing again only long enough to take her hand, lead her back inside. Those warm wintry scents of pine and cinnamon engulfed her senses as he quickly flicked off a lamp, leaving the room aglow with only the lights on the Christmas tree.

As he eased her back on the couch, she couldn't deny that

he'd made it as perfect as the situation allowed for. Somehow dim lighting made it easier—more like a dream. The colored glow and scents made it feel safe, romantic. If someone had ever described this scene to her and claimed she'd think it perfect, she'd have thought they were crazy. But she was learning that life was all about perspective—and as Jace arced his body over hers, their legs intertwining like vines in the swamp as he began to rain sweet kisses on her neck, it was perfect. As she let her eyes fall shut, let the smells of Christmas surround her, let those kisses saturate her senses, it was perfect. And when he lowered his weight onto her enough that she felt the evidence of his desire hard and full against her hip—oh Lord, that was perfect, too.

But wait, no, not totally perfect that part—because she ached to feel it somewhere else. Enough that she set her shyness aside just long enough to ease her hands down his sides—under the open flannel shirt he wore but over the tee beneath—and slowly onto his hips, to shift their bodies just slightly until the hardness behind his zipper pressed squarely into the softness under hers.

Oh. Yes. Now *that* was perfect. A soft, high moan escaped her.

And it drew a low groan from him.

And she began to move beneath him—her body acting almost of its own volition, seeking that heady pleasure that often stole a person's sense and was certainly absconding with hers now.

He moved against her in the same way, a primal dance of simulated sex, their labored breath making her wish for Christmas music to mask it, making her feel their animal instincts even more.

His hands came onto her breasts then—gently at first, his thumbs stroking her nipples through her top and bra, heightening her pleasure, taking her closer to the peak her desire was rising toward. Her breath grew thready, her whole body warming from the inside out.

He kneaded her breasts more firmly then, rasping, almost trembling, and again she could feel him holding back for her, trying to make this something more soft than hard, more sweet than wild. She was stuck between needing the first and hungering for the second in a way she almost didn't understand. She'd always enjoyed sex—but for her, it had never been an urgent act, a frenzied thing you rush to. And right now, an unfamiliar part of her suffered that frenzy.

Yet she was wise enough to know that the gentleness he'd offered was the right course, so she undulated against him, drank in his touches, longed for more but let him guide her. She wasn't good at trusting—but for this moment she would trust Jason Rose.

Soon his hands began gathering the fabric of her top in his fists—he was pulling it up, wanting it off her. "Lift your arms," he murmured, and she acquiesced, letting him remove it, toss it aside.

A glance down left her unduly pleased that today of all random days she'd worn her pink bra with the rhinestones rather than a plainer one. It had simply come up in the rotation—but now seemed like fate smiling on her, making her feel feminine and sexy and pretty when she'd least expected to want to feel that way.

He smiled at the sight of the bra, too. "I saw this on the day we met. I like seeing it *on* you better."

"Do you want...to take it off me?" She scarcely knew where the words had come from. The animal part of her, she supposed.

"God, yes, honey," he rasped—and she drew in her breath with anticipation as he eased his hands under her on the couch and smoothly unhooked the bra, the elastic band loosening around her.

When he drew it away with a low moan, her heart beat like a drum. The way he looked at her felt like being touched, creating a pleasure that reverberated at the crux of her thighs. Again, an urge toward frenzy, needing him *now*, *fast*, *hard*. But she simply blew out a breath and remembered that this was new, and it should be scarier than it felt right now, and even if she wasn't big on letting men control her, she'd somehow assigned him control of *this*, so she resolved to let him have it.

The second his mouth closed around her turgid nipple, a sob of pleasure erupted from her throat. And then he was suckling her, turning that pleasure thicker and heavier, and her hands were in his hair, on his shoulders—forgetting the fear of touching now that they were more intimate.

And then he was fumbling free from his flannel shirt, stopping his ministrations just long enough to shed the tee as well. More flesh revealed, more skin touching hers—intimate and exciting and rippling with heat. His shoulders were broad, his arms leanly muscled and sporting the pale tan you'd expect from a southern man in winter.

Down below, he worked at the button on her blue jeans, and then the zipper, starting to push them down. He did the same with his until they were both kicking free of the denim. Closer, so much closer now, nearly naked together, and she became aware that in trying to hold back herself, she was gently scraping the tips of her fingernails along his shoulders in lieu of grabbing, kneading, holding on too tight.

The next thing she knew, his mouth was back at her breast, his erection at the front of her panties, and everything inside her pulsed with fever, pushing her to move against him, harder, harder—and she quit caring if she held on too tight, gripping his shoulders, wrapping her legs around his as she moved beneath him in hot, rhythmic circles. Until she plunged headlong into an orgasm that broke over her with the power of a tidal wave, making her cry out as the pleasure rolled through her and over her, consuming her.

"Oh—God," she said, almost embarrassed as she came back to herself. She felt like a teenager. "I'm not sure that was supposed to happen yet." They were both still in underwear.

But above her, Jace simply gave her a sexy, satisfied grin. "Doesn't matter when it happens, honey—just as long as it does."

She bit her lip as she gazed up into his clear blue eyes, still recovering—and at the same time still yearning for more.

His breath was heavy, labored, as he kissed her neck and then murmured against her skin, "But now I want inside you." His fingers curled into the elastic of her panties to begin pulling them down.

Still a little breathless, she lifted, letting him remove them —and for the first time it occurred to her to ask, "Do you have—"

"Of course." He reached for the jeans that had recently hit the floor, drawing a worn leather wallet from a back pocket. Despite her climax, her body remained at a fever pitch, hungry for what came next. She watched as he ripped open a foil packet and withdrew a condom, then rose above her on his knees to put it on.

Even in the low glow of the Christmas lights, she was taken aback by the sight of him that way—large and erect— and it made her body feel all the more ready for him. She blew out a breath. This was not what she'd expected—any of it. A man. His persistence. His kindness. And now his sex.

She followed the instinct to part her legs, open herself to him. It excited her when he studied her there. It excited her more when he bent back over her, braced his hands on her bare hips, and began to push his way inside her.

The fit was snug—she clenched her teeth as he entered as gently as possible.

But then he was in, all the way, and she released a trembling breath as the fullness spread through her. A sigh of pure pleasure echoed up into the pine-scented air.

"So tight," he murmured hot against her skin—and she lifted against him, wanting him to thrust.

And then thrust he did—slow, deep, making her feel every inch of him sliding in, sliding out. Low moans left her. And then he began to groan, too. He still struggled to hold back, she could tell. She suspected these slow, measured strokes weren't his usual way of making love to a woman. And yet they were delivered as masterfully as if he were a bow and she a violin.

They moved together in that hot, slow rhythm until it took over her every thought, her every sense. She no longer pondered anything that was happening—but was simply a part of it, soaking it up, floating in a deep sexual connection she'd never expected to have. She closed her eyes, let go of all fear, let go of anything but how good it felt to connect, to live, to experience everything humans were put here to experience. She hadn't felt so alive in…well, she wasn't sure how long. And it didn't matter. All that mattered was that she was living. Even after everything she'd been through, she was living.

Jace's breath came ragged as he said, "I can't go slow anymore, honey," and began to drive into her harder, faster. Each plunge rocked her to her core with a new, rougher sort of pleasure—until he moaned, "I'm coming—I'm coming in you."

They both cried out as he did.

And as he rested his head on her shoulder, spent, three words filled her brain. *Best laid plans.*

She wasn't sure how she'd feel tomorrow, but tonight she was so very glad they'd changed.

✳

HALF AN HOUR later they still lay together naked, covered by an old quilt sized for a child's bed that she'd found in a closet and draped across the back of the couch.

Propped on one elbow beside her, Jace grazed his fingertips down her arm, lowered a kiss to her shoulder, then peered into her eyes. "Do you want to tell me yet?"

She met his gaze. And didn't have to ask what he was talking about. It was the enormous elephant in the room. It *had* been since the moment they'd met.

And no, she didn't want to tell him.

But she owed him more than she was giving. The man deserved an explanation.

"It's hard to know where to begin."

"Start anywhere," he told her, "and I'll catch up."

"Maybe it's easier," she mused, "to start at the end than at the beginning." Then she took a deep breath. "I left a man who I think was going to kill me. And I'm still afraid he'll find me and pull it off."

CHAPTER TEN

*S*he watched Jace's eyes go wide as his body tensed alongside hers. "The hell he will. Not as long as I'm around."

And maybe those words should have made her feel safe, grateful, but...well, there was no way he could know all she'd endured. And she needed to make him understand.

"His name is Craig and I met him three years ago, shortly after my mother died." She explained then about her mom's lymphoma, that they'd lived in Indianapolis where Shelby had been born and raised. "But following her death, I got a new job in Chicago and moved. Higher salary, a step up in the ad world, and Mom's illness and death was, frankly, expensive. The job seemed like a good way to start paying off those bills and I thought a whole new life in a new city would help me move past the loss. When the job offer came along, it seemed like fate smiling on me."

She told Jace then about meeting Craig, whose law practice represented her advertising firm, their offices being in the same building and located just one floor below. "He was handsome, accomplished, attentive, and pretty much swept me off my feet." She traveled back in time to those early days with Craig when she'd been head over heels in love. "Those first few weeks were...like magic. I thought he was the man my mother had always told me I would find. He seemed perfect. And he made the relationship move fast—which at the time flattered me. He wanted to see me every day, and every night, and he was always stopping into my office, and bringing me flowers. Every woman in the agency was envious, and I understood why—he seemed like a dream, like the perfect catch, and was totally devoted to me."

Jace's eyes narrowed. "How on earth did it go from that to...well, what you just told me?"

She sighed. It was a good question. And the answer was, "He made me trust him completely, then let me depend on him completely, and then manipulated my entire life until I had no control over it at all.

"First, he started insisting I let him help with the funeral debt, and credit card bills that had gotten run up. Initially, I said no, but he paid my bills anyway, often without my knowledge. And after that...well, it was easy to accept the help when he pushed it—and he got intimately involved in every aspect of my life quickly. I was in a weak place, trying to climb out of the darkness. And when a guy seems perfect and you're in love, you don't see any reason not to let him in." She shook her head, remembering her naïveté. Or had it just been bad luck? Either way, she was naïve no longer.

"That was when the trouble started. He began trying to control my social life—acting put out if I wanted to have dinner with a woman I'd started making friends with in the office, or angry if he saw me talking to another man, even one I worked with. It started out subtly, but escalated into really unreasonable behavior. And it was confusing, since I cared for him and we were already in a very established relationship, practically engaged. It was a side of him I hadn't seen, and I tried to explain it away—tell myself he was stressed at work or something, that it was an aberration."

She pursed her lips, uneasy at revisiting her history with Craig. But she'd barely scratched the surface in explaining the situation to Jace. She glanced up at the man next to her. "Only it wasn't an aberration. It just got worse and worse. By this time, he'd talked me into giving up my apartment and moving in with him, so breaking up wasn't easy—and every time I told him I wanted to, he would either fall all over himself promising to make me happy or he'd get irrationally angry. Either way, I began to realize I was trapped.

"What made it even worse was being in a new city. I hadn't made any real friends yet—only work relationships that had produced some casual acquaintances. So there was no one to turn to for help who didn't already think Craig was a great guy, and no one but me to witness what was happening behind closed doors. And I was still fairly fragile after losing my mom."

"No dad? Other family?" Jace asked.

She shook her head against a throw pillow. "I never knew my dad—all I have from him is his last name. He got my mom pregnant and abandoned her, so she raised me on her own. And she was a great mother. We were close—two peas in a pod. My grandparents moved from here to Columbia when my mom was in high school and they passed away when *I* was in high school. And I have an uncle in Florida, but he's always lived far away so I've never known him well. Though this house is technically his, and he's a nice man—but we weren't in close touch and he's not someone I would think to turn to for help." Until wanting to come here, that was. Maybe she should have turned to Uncle Gary sooner. But that was water under the bridge.

"Then things got really crazy—shockingly crazy," she went on to Jace. The hard part was coming. Well, harder than what had come before anyway. "When I was sick with the flu for two weeks, he quit my job for me."

Next to her, Jace blinked, then lowered his chin, clearly stunned. "He what?"

"You heard me right. He told my boss I'd decided I wanted to stay at home and do charity work, and that I resigned. And the thing is—people think Craig is a great guy. He's totally charming. He and my boss were friends—they golfed together. So my boss took him at his word—he made it seem plausible. And somehow—unbelievably—I suddenly just didn't have a job anymore. Or much of anything. He'd taken over my finances. He'd taken over everything. And then…" She stopped, drew a deep breath, because even now the memory made her blanch. "A few months ago he started locking me in our condo."

"*What?*" She appreciated how aghast Jace sounded. She was *still* aghast. "How the hell did he do *that?*"

Another sigh left her at the troubling memory. "He had a high tech security system that, when he set it a certain way, could only be unlocked—on either side of the door—electronically. So he'd go to work and lock me in, and then claim it was an accident. But it happened over and over—and I knew it *wasn't* an accident." She paused, steeled herself. "That was the worst feeling I'd ever had. Being trapped that way. It was a high-rise on Lakeshore Drive, so there was no getting out any other way but the door. If there'd been a fire or something…well, it was just an awful feeling."

"I can imagine. I'm so sorry, honey."

"And even when he didn't lock me in…I didn't know how to find help. Like I said, I didn't have friends—and the people I *did* know were *his* friends. Our money had become intermingled and he'd arranged it so I didn't have access to much of it. He'd pretty much stolen the life I'd been trying to build and commandeered it for his own. He was trying to turn me into some kind of Stepford Wife or something—wanting me to be nothing but doting arm candy. Wanting me to cook for him, clean for him. Getting angry if the bed was unmade or there were crumbs on the counter."

"He sounds like a lunatic," Jace suggested.

"He *is* a lunatic," she assured him, unduly pleased that Jace had chosen the very word to describe Craig that always came to mind for her. It was somehow validating. "But he's the kind of lunatic who has everyone snowed. Everyone loves him. Before it was done, I had no acquaintances who weren't in his circle. Well, other than one woman I'd worked with, a receptionist who I ran into at the grocery store after my job was gone. She expressed her surprise, and little by little I ended up telling her what had happened. When I decided to leave, she was my confidante—even let me know ahead of time when Craig and the ad firm execs had a business dinner so I could plan to leave that morning and get that much more of a head start."

"Terrible as all that is, though, honey—think I missed something. The part about you thinking he was...gonna kill you?"

Jace looked almost as if he still thought he'd misheard that part. And she wished that were true. She still couldn't believe it herself. "His mother once told me he'd had a fiancée who died—just a year or so before we met. He never wanted to talk about it—always glossed over the details and led me believe it was just too painful for him. But apparently she fell off a balcony in an apartment they shared together. And he was home at the time. And though it doesn't seem like anyone ever suspected him, the whole thing sounded a little too unsolved and mysterious for my liking.

"So a couple of months ago, out of desperation because he was starting to seem more and more easily agitated, I started looking into his personal past. And I found out that in college he had a girlfriend who fell down a flight of stairs and died. And I reached out the girl's sister on social media, and she told me she'd always thought Craig had done it, had pushed her. She said he started out charming, but turned into a control freak, and that when her sister wouldn't be controlled, he couldn't stand it and ended up killing her.

"And that was it. As soon as I heard that, that there was a second mysterious death of a girlfriend, I knew I had to find a way out. And sure, I could have gone back to Indy, but he'd have found me there—I'm sure it's the first place he looked. He'd have likely charmed anyone who was trying to help me and that's a chance I couldn't take.

"I decided to come here, keep to myself, and not tell anyone anything. Maybe what I did seems extreme, but I just wanted to get as far away from him as possible, as fast as possible—come what may.

"And who knows—maybe he's not looking for me at all. Or maybe he looked and has given up by now. I have no idea how his crazy, manipulative, entitled mind works—maybe he's already on the hunt for the next girl who'd better let herself be controlled or else. But I didn't want to take any chances. None at all.

"One morning after he left for work, I packed as much as I could efficiently move, drove to the bank and withdrew twelve hundred dollars—which drained the joint checking account, since he keeps the bulk of the money in other places I didn't have access to—then headed south.

"And that's it—the whole ugly, crazy story." She'd talked for a long time, uninterrupted. She'd needed to just spew it all out, get it off her chest in one shot. But now that she'd finished, she lifted her gaze to Jace. "Do you think it was insane of me? To leave everything behind that way?"

She valued how thunderstruck he appeared. "If you feared for your life, no. I mean..." He shook his head. "I've never...not had family to turn to. I can't imagine what that was like—to deal with that completely alone. I'm so damn sorry you had to go through that, honey."

She thought back through all her dealings with Jace so far. "Now maybe you can begin to understand why...why..."

He tilted his head. "Why you're so damn bad at accepting help? Yeah. I guess so."

"I just can't become beholden to anyone, can't let anyone give me so much that I feel I owe them anything. Maybe I'm too paranoid about it, but it's ingrained in me now."

"Well, something like that would get in your head pretty deep. I just wish..."

"What?"

"That I knew how to convince you I'm a good guy, that it's okay to accept *my* help."

"Well, the truth is...I kind of know that you are," she confessed. "Only...every time I tell myself that, I remember that he was a nice guy in the beginning, too." She flashed a sad look up at him. "This is why I keep telling you I can't go down that road, can't date or see anyone."

He raised his eyebrows, teased her. "Then I guess this officially make us friends with benefits?"

"I'm...not sure *what* this makes us, to be honest."

He tilted his head, gave her a small smile. "Do you realize I don't even know your last name?"

She felt silly. "I'm sorry I've been so secretive. I just haven't wanted to share anything about myself the least bit traceable." She shook her head. "I didn't even like putting it on my job application at Pete's, dumb as that sounds."

"It doesn't sound dumb. It sounds like...a natural response to what you've been through."

"My last name is...Scott." Stupid, but it was still hard to say. So she made herself do it again. "I'm Shelby Scott."

His smile grew. "It's nice to meet you, Shelby Scott."

She glanced down at their nakedness, their bodies still touching. "I don't usually have sex before introducing myself."

"Me neither. Most of the time." His grin faded uncertainly.

And she voiced her next thought out loud. "I have the feeling you get around. Maybe have a *lot* of friends with benefits."

He shrugged. "Sometimes. Yeah. Maybe. But..."

"But...what? I'm your new favorite?"

He laughed. "Well, you're my only—right now. That's what I was gonna say—that you're my only."

"And why is that?"

He shrugged. "My life got a little reorganized earlier this year—guess I'm just still letting the pieces fall into place, and haven't been much in the mood for..."

"Benefits," she finished for him.

And he laughed. "Yeah. Benefits. So thank you for changing that, honey." Another chuckle. "Is it okay to call you honey now? Have we passed that mile marker yet?"

She cast him a sideways grin. "I suppose. I've been letting it go lately, in case you haven't noticed."

"I have," he confirmed. "I took it as a good sign, and I was right." Another cute grin. And God, she liked him. So much. Too much. He was just...easy to be with. Well, when he wasn't forcing help on her. But despite all her wariness, she was starting to drop her guard with him a little, starting to trust. Just a bit. Just a smidge. He was hard *not* to trust.

And again, she'd have said that about Craig in the early days, too. Other people who knew Craig would surely swear to it even now. She imagined he was telling their friends how she'd just up and left him with no warning, that he was heartbroken, and they were probably all too busy comforting him to ever suspect he was the bad guy here.

"So do *you* want to tell *me?*" she asked.

"Tell you what?"

"Why you haven't been in the mood for benefits? How your life changed? What pieces are falling into place?"

For some reason, the question caught Jace off-guard. Maybe because, in his mind, he'd been an open book with her, and she was the one swirling and whirling in mystery. But he guessed he really hadn't had occasion to tell her much about himself—most of their interactions had been him offering help to her and her trying to refuse it.

"Does it have anything to do with selling Christmas trees?" she asked.

The question made him smile. Because it was so damn accurate. "As a matter of fact, Shelby honey, it does."

CHAPTER ELEVEN

*B*ut then he flashed a doubtful expression. "Although…nobody's locking me in a house or trying to kill me, so my situation might not sound too dire in comparison."

"Good," she told him. "I have enough dire for both of us, so if your problems are a walk in the park next to mine, I'll take it."

He reached up, scratched his forehead. "Tell you the truth, they seem like *nothing* next to yours." What had felt world-rocking and life-altering to him a few minutes ago suddenly seemed like small beans.

"Everything's relative," she reminded him. Which he knew. But he admired her for remaining aware of that after all she'd been through. He was still digesting it—the loss of her mother to a terrible disease, the pressure of dealing with debt, the courage to move to a new city on her own, and then getting connected with a psycho who'd made her feel trapped and afraid. It was a lot. No wonder she'd decided to just run away from it all.

"True, but for the record, my life is suddenly seeming pretty damn peachy after everything you just said."

She made an impatient face. "Tell me. It's only fair."

"Okay, okay." He met her gaze. "It's about my family's business—now *my* business."

She nodded. "Keep going."

"My whole life my parents ran a nursery on the edge of town. And me, I drove an eighteen-wheeler for the last ten years—did long haul trucking all over the country. And that may not sound like some kind of jet set life, but for me, it was. I wanted to see the country, from one side to the other, corner to corner, top to bottom.

"When I was a kid, there were two things I was into. Race cars—had the idea I was gonna drive one someday—and maps. I wasn't a straight A student, but at geography I was a whiz. I learned about different places and wanted to see them all. And driving a truck seemed like a way to do two things I loved. A big rig isn't exactly a race car, but at least it's got wheels and kept me moving. So I worked at the nursery as a teenager, saved up my money, got my CDL license, and bought myself a truck.

"And like I said, I know it's not glamorous travel—but for me, it was an adventure, and freedom. The freedom to do what I wanted, go where I wanted, see places and things I wouldn't get to any other way. Always something new—new town, new city, new bridge to cross, new stretch of highway. I love this town, and I love my family—but that freedom was important to me. It was a life I loved, and I made good money, too.

"I never planned to do it forever…but I planned to do it for as long as it felt good to me. And I wasn't ready to be done with it."

"And then?" she asked.

"My parents decided to retire. And for me to take over the family business." He knew his dry tone said it all. "My two brothers have businesses of their own—Rick has the bar and Tanner heads up a construction company—but to my mom and dad, *my* business wasn't really a business, not one you couldn't just give up. They didn't understand that it's actually damn hard to make good money on the road, that not everybody who starts it does as well as I did. And they didn't get that they were asking me to change my entire life just because they were ready to change theirs."

"But sounds like you did it anyway," she said.

"Yep."

"Why?"

Jace thought about that. "Lotta reasons," he told her. "Like I said, it meant something to them. It meant a *lot* to them. It's a thriving family business—generations of customers rely on Rose's Nursery for their flowers and their shrubs and their—"

"Christmas trees?" she cut in.

He grinned softly. "Yeah, Christmas trees." Then went on. "Rick told me I should say no, that they'd have to understand it was my choice and not theirs. But in the end, I just couldn't let 'em down. Because I love 'em. And I didn't want to see the business *they'd* built suddenly stop existing. I guess the truth is that I value it, too. Maybe more than I've wanted to admit."

"That's really nice," she said softly, surprising him somehow.

He drew back slightly. "Nice that I let someone else make my decisions for me?"

She shrugged. "Nicer than the way I ended up letting someone make decisions for *me*. It's nice because you're doing it out of love. And respect and appreciation for what they created."

He let out a sigh. All that was true. "But even though I value the place and don't mind the work...well, guess I thought I'd get used to the change, that it wouldn't be a big deal. And the truth is that I really miss...I don't know, just the sense of freedom I felt behind the wheel every day."

"Maybe," she began, "you just need to find...the next big thing in your life. Like *I'm* slowly trying to do. Is there anything you want to do that you haven't? Anything big?"

This time it was he who shrugged, then chuckled. "Well, there's that race car driving thing. But it's a little late for that."

"Is it?" she shot back at him, eyebrows raised.

"Well, most drivers start young. Even guys who drive at small tracks start young—grow into it, learn the ropes early."

"Most doesn't mean all," she said. "I mean, if it's something you think you'd enjoy and be good at, couldn't you get into it now? Look into how to get started."

Jace took that in. There'd been a time, back in high school, when he'd seriously wanted to race. His dad and grandpa had often taken him and his brothers to regional dirt tracks to watch stock, modified, and late model racing. If the wind was blowing the wrong way at the dirt track on a hot night, they'd all come home caked with a heavy layer of dust thrown up by the cars sliding sideways through the turns, but he'd loved it—couldn't get enough of it. He'd wanted to be one of those guys flying around that oval, accelerating to top speed, drafting off other cars until he could find a way to snake past first one and then another.

"My parents would both have heart attacks," he said. Looking back, that was one reason he'd never gotten to pursue it. He couldn't blame his parents for playing the "it's dangerous" card on the occasions he'd brought it up. They'd nixed the idea quick—and he'd moved on to the notion of trucking as a more practical way to feed his need for freedom behind the wheel.

But Shelby seemed unfazed. "You took over their business for them—if you want to do something for *you* now, they'll just have to get with the program."

He let out a laugh, liking her way of thinking. He loved his parents, but just because he'd sacrificed his career for them didn't mean he had to keep *on* sacrificing things. And while the very idea of getting into racing at this late date in his life sounded a little crazy, the notion excited him instantly. Same as when he was a boy, when it had seemed like something that could really be possible.

"I know some people," he heard himself think out loud. "A few guys who own or drive race cars, or both. I guess I could always stop by their places, see what they can tell me about it."

"I think you should do it. After all, what's the harm?"

She made a good point—there was no harm at all. He and Tanner sometimes still made the trek to regional speedways —it was an interest that had stayed in Jace's blood—so if nothing else, he'd learn a little more about the racing life. "Alright, Shelby Scott, you talked me into it."

THE NEXT MORNING, Shelby stood on her front porch letting Jason Rose kiss her goodbye under the mistletoe she'd unwittingly hung there. Part of her still couldn't believe she'd allowed this to happen—she'd never expected to want a man to touch her again so soon, if ever—but she couldn't deny that it had been an amazing night.

She also couldn't believe she'd told him...everything. Once she'd started, the words had spilled out like a tipped over watering can. Her secrets, which she'd planned to *keep* secret, were suddenly out in the open.

"Take care of yourself, Shelby honey," he said, "and I'll see you soon."

Part of her wanted to know *how* soon, like a smitten teenager who can't get enough, who wants to be surrounded by that chemistry and electricity all the time. But a bigger part of her appreciated that he was being casual and vague about it. Since that was still what she needed to feel safe— relationships that were loose, distant, nothing serious. And she almost wanted to thank him for giving her that—but part of backing away from the intimacy of last night was, indeed, distance. It was following his lead and putting more of it between them right now.

"Sounds good," she said. *That* was casual, distant. Even if her heart beat too hard and she already missed him the moment he descended the steps and strode toward his truck.

"Jace," she said. It had just come out. No decision. Just impulse.

He stopped, looked back.

"Thank you. For the tree. And...for everything."

As a warm smile unfurled across his handsome face, she knew he felt just how strongly her gratitude ran. "My pleasure, Shelby Scott."

She stood leaning against a weathered porch rail, wearing only a thin T-shirt that reached the tops of her thighs, and watched him go. And as his truck rumbled away, she felt... lighter. Lighter than she had since coming here.

Stepping back in through the old screen door, her eyes fell on the Christmas tree that hadn't been there yesterday. But it was more than just a Christmas tree. It was as if... warmth, kindness, and hope all dripped from the boughs along with the angels she and Jace had hung there.

The last thing she needed in her life was a hot, sexy man.

But, despite herself, she was so glad she'd found one. She felt less alone in the world, and given that she'd underestimated just how hard "alone" could be, she wasn't sorry she'd let down her walls a little. She wasn't sorry she'd let herself trust a little.

CHAPTER TWELVE

*J*ace had never done so much for a woman, gone
to so much trouble for a woman, let alone one
he barely knew. Maybe it was because she was
clearly in need. He'd never seen himself as a rescuer, the kind
of guy drawn to a damsel in distress—but there was something about her that just left him wanting to…make things
easier for her. And now that he understood what had
brought her here with so little, he wanted to help even more.

That was what led him back down Cypress Stump Road
after leaving work the next day. Part of him feared it was
too soon; maybe he should let her have her space. He hated
what she'd been through and he understood now why she
had trouble accepting his help. But winter was looming,
even in low country—and much as he might just want to
rip her clothes off and have his way with her in the front
yard, and on the porch, and up against the wall, and every
other place he could think of, he'd come for a practical
reason.

He didn't get an answer when he knocked on the door.
And a walk around the house revealed that the bicycle was

gone. Either she'd ridden into town or she'd taken it to Salty Pete's today and wasn't back yet.

So he found a good spot next to the house and began unloading the firewood he'd brought. He wasn't sure if the house had heat, and she might need that fireplace now that nights were getting chilly. Of course, he'd have to make sure she knew how to build a fire and wouldn't burn the place down.

And when she still hadn't returned after he'd finished unloading, he took an old wooden ladder he'd seen lying along the back foundation of the house, tested it for strength, then used it to climb up on the roof. This whole place needed an overhaul, but the cottage had solid bones, and the roof seemed to hold his weight. Having carried up an old broom, he headed toward the slanted brick chimney and peered down into it.

Pulling a flashlight from the toolbelt he wore, he took a closer look and found the view actually wasn't too bad. One old bird's next, within arm's reach, so he removed it, and he spied some dirt and debris along the inner walls, which he knocked down into the fireplace with the broom.

Next, he attached some chicken wire over the top with a bungee cord. Wouldn't look pretty, but it would keep birds and any other pests out until he could install a screen. Looked like there'd once been one, but it was broken. Maybe just recently, given that the house didn't seem to be overrun by vermin.

He'd just tossed the broom over the side of the house to the ground and started backing carefully down the ladder when a sharp voice cut through the late day silence. "What the hell are you doing up there?"

He turned to peer down at the pretty woman standing below him, glaring up. "Nice to see you, too. I cleaned out your chimney."

She let out a loud sigh. "And what the hell is *this?*"

As he continued backing down the ladder, he followed her gaze and said, "Firewood. The nights are getting colder."

There was no missing how irritated she looked when he reached the ground. "I don't care," she said. "You shouldn't be doing this."

"I shouldn't?" Damn, he'd been right about giving her space. He'd hoped what they'd shared would have left her more at ease, but apparently not.

"No. You have to stop. It's too much."

Jace sighed. "I was afraid you'd react like this."

Her eyebrows shot up. "And still you did it anyway?"

Okay, he saw her point and regretted it now. "I was hoping I was wrong. So I apologize. But like I told you, honey, it's a safety issue. If you'd built a fire before I did this, you might have sent the whole place up in smoke."

She blew out a huffing sound, looking incredulous. And too damn kissable. "Even so, you know now why I feel this way, why I can't keep accepting your generosity."

He gave his head a pointed tilt. "But you can. I thought we'd agreed on that. At least sort of." He met her gaze, getting more serious. "I'd never hurt you, honey."

Yet she didn't miss a beat. "*He* said that."

"Oh." Damn. That guy had done such a number on her. The bastard was just lucky he was all the way up in Chicago. Jace drew in a breath, tried to push down his response and get back to the matter at hand. "What can I do to make you trust me, Shelby?"

She pursed her lips, and if he wasn't mistaken, appeared to be seriously thinking through it. Which was at least a lot better than he'd been getting from her before yesterday. After a moment, she said, "Take it one day at a time. And... quit showering me with gifts."

He shifted his weight from one workboot to the other.

On one hand, he didn't want to push her now that he knew about her past. But on the other, his parents had raised him to be practical—and hell, he worried about her. "I wouldn't call them gifts," he explained gently. "I see it more as lending you useful stuff that's sitting in my garage."

Then he headed back around the front of the cottage, toward his truck, the tailgate already lowered. He could see in his peripheral vision that she'd followed. Reaching up into the bed, he lifted out an old TV. "Like this. Won't get many channels—just the local ones out of Charleston if you're lucky once I stick an antenna on the roof."

"I can't accept that," she said, stubborn as ever.

So he changed his strategy. "Okay, fine. You don't want it, I'll put it back in the garage. Even if I'd feel like you're safer out here having access to the news. And sitcoms."

Her eyes widened in doubt. "You'll feel safer if I can watch sitcoms?"

He tossed her a smile. "Yeah. Seems too quiet and lonely out here to me. Might need something to make you laugh. If you do, sitcoms. And hey," he continued, taking yet another new tack, "if you have a TV, maybe I won't feel like you need my company so much and I'll leave you alone more." He ended on a wink. "But like I said, if you don't want it, I'll take it back. Far be it from me to push an old TV set on someone who doesn't want one."

"Where did it come from?" she asked.

"The TV? My parents downsized when they retired, and a bunch of their junk ended up at my place. It's a piece of crap that was in my dad's workshop—doesn't get a great picture."

"And you're being honest about all that?"

The question drove home for him what a hard time she had believing...anyone—about anything, it seemed. "Trust me—it's give it to you or put it in the trash heap. Does that make you feel better?"

He watched as her expression slowly relaxed, even though he could tell she was trying to stay tough. "Yes, actually," she said, her voice softer now.

"Thank God. I get tired of arguing with you. We'll find a place to put it in your living room, then I'll hook up the antenna." Though he stopped, thought, and added, *"If that's okay with you."*

She pulled in a breath, let it back out—and relented. "Yes —it's okay."

He nodded, pleased. Pleased that he was remembering to be more considerate and that she was accepting it. "Then after that, I'll teach you to start a fire—since I'm guessing you don't know how."

She sighed, looking a little forlorn now. "That would be a correct guess."

"Stick with me, baby," he said, offering up a reassuring grin, "and I'll have you building fires in no time."

Half an hour later, he'd attached the antenna and TV, which indeed only picked up a couple of local stations. And in truth, even as hard as it was to accept so much giving of so many things, Shelby was elated to have the TV.

It was one of the things she'd lamented not planning for. Not because she was a TV-aholic or anything, but because the house *was* too quiet at night, and so many times she'd wished for the simple feeling of connection to the outside world a TV could provide. It *would* be nice to watch the local news, and even, as he'd suggested, a few comedies. In some ways, she'd started learning to appreciate the silence and solitude here, but in another, this was a convenience she would welcome.

Turned out that fire-building was frustratingly harder than she'd expected, but she tried her best. Along with everything else, he'd brought supplies for the task. And as they knelt before the hearth together, as she watched his hands arranging kindling and firewood, watched his eyes as he concentrated, his mouth as he instructed her—she realized just how much she wanted him again. In every way.

Just look at all he's doing for me. Look how much he cares.

And yet, what a frightening feeling. Because it was so very similar to what she'd once felt for Craig. In those early days. When he, too, had seemed so very considerate, like his only wish in the world was to take away her burdens and make her happy.

So you have to keep those walls up. You can't let them down.

Okay, maybe having sex with him had been letting them down. But there were emotional walls to be breached, too— and what she had almost let herself feel here, that rush of warmth and gratitude and desire, that could still be kept at bay.

So that was what she did. Kept it at bay. Learned to build the fire. Stopped looking at him. Tried like hell not to feel the flutter in her stomach just from his very nearness, his very maleness and ruggedness.

Don't fall for this guy. Just don't do it.

By the time a good fire roared in the hearth, darkness had fallen. She was still trying to get used to how early it came this time of year on the East Coast—it felt like night when it was only late afternoon. Like night, when it somehow got easier to succumb to urges to kiss, or touch, or fall into bed with a sexy man.

Please don't tempt me, Jace, because I'm not sure I can resist your charms. Letting herself be seduced last night had been... well, huge. Huger even now because already having gone there with him suddenly made it seem all the more crazy to push him away. And yet, if she let it happen over and over again, she wasn't sure how she'd keep up *any* walls. They were already crumbling too much.

"Okay," he said, pushing to his feet. "TV on, fire burning—I think my work here is done."

She nodded. "Seems that way." She didn't meet his eyes, even though that took effort now. He had *great* eyes. "And it's late, so…" Of course, it wasn't late at all, but the words had tumbled out on impulse to urge his departure.

He grinned, clearly getting the message. "So I'll leave you in peace," he said, then lowered his voice. "Even if I'd much rather leave you naked in bed."

She didn't reply, *couldn't* reply. Since she wanted him naked, too, and the longing tightened her chest. Even as she ushered him toward the door.

"Thank you," he told her.

She blinked, surprised. "For what?"

"Accepting my help. It'll put my mind at ease knowing you're warm and…informed." He let out a short laugh at his rhyme.

"You're welcome," she said. "But that's it. No more—okay?"

Instead of answering that, however, he motioned back to the TV—where the evening news was on—and said, "You heard about the storm, right?"

She turned toward the screen to see a meteorologist pointing to a swirling mass on a map, currently over the Atlantic. "Um, no."

Jace just shook his head. "See, this is why you need a TV. Tropical storm headed toward the Carolina coast. Sometimes we get a late one like this, even after hurricane season. Shouldn't be bad, but some heavy rains predicted for a couple days, blowing in tomorrow night. So be sure you have food, water, anything else you need." Then he glanced upward. "And damn, hope that antenna holds. I didn't consider the storm when I put it up."

"I'm sure it'll be fine," she said. Mainly thinking that she

118

needed him out the door, now. Because everything about him—right down to his worries for the antenna—made her want him more. Storm, food and water—she'd deal with all that tomorrow. Right now she needed the hot man in front of her to leave and take all the heat he generated with him.

"But if it's not," he went on, "I'll get back up there and secure it better. Maybe get Tanner to come help."

Oh boy. Now he was enlisting his brother in Project Save Shelby, too? "Oh my God—no more, Jace. Seriously. Okay?"

"Then I guess you don't want these Christmas cookies my mother made?" He gestured to a festive tin with a cartoonish Santa on the lid that he'd apparently carried in at some point and placed on the mantel without her noticing.

She let out a sigh. "Well…those I'll take." She couldn't see a reason to pass up homemade cookies, after all. *But don't let yourself feel anything over them. Over his thoughtfulness in bringing them. Over wondering who he told his mother they were for. Don't feel anything at all.* "Now goodbye," she said, going so far as to physically take his arm and lead him to the door.

"Goodbye, honey," he said—then planted an oh-so-delicious kiss on her surprised but acceptant lips before letting the screen door slam behind him.

JACE DROVE up Cypress Stump Road with the taste of her kiss fresh and warm on his mouth. Damn, he was into her. And it was hard to hold back just now—hard not to follow the male instincts that made him want her beneath him in bed, writhing and panting and moaning as she had the night before.

But he was trying like hell to respect her boundaries. As much as he could anyway. He couldn't help making her safety and comfort his first priority. Now that he understood what she'd been through, though, it was at least easier to understand her behavior.

And it was frustrating to know she didn't completely trust him yet, but at least for today he had managed to exercise some patience. One day at a time, she'd said. And she'd practically pushed him out the door a few minutes ago. But she'd kissed him back, despite herself. And maybe tomorrow, or the next day, she *wouldn't* push him out. Maybe soon enough she'd be inviting him in, all the way in, where he wanted to be with her.

He still didn't quite understand the depth of his desire for her—but he'd take that one day at a time, too.

Heading for home, he thought of leftovers in his fridge from a recent family meal—they'd be his dinner tonight. Then a hot shower and maybe a little TV. But as he approached Mossy Branch Road, he found himself turning unexpectedly onto it. It was literally "the long way home," connecting up with another couple of roads that led to his house, but making for a much less direct route than going through town.

Though when he saw the lights on in Rowdy Cutler's garage, he knew full well why he'd come this way.

Pulling his truck over into the gravel that fronted the roadside garage, its door wide open, he spied Rowdy bent over the hood of a late model modified Camaro, painted blue and white, with a red number eleven on the side. Rowdy, a skinny red-haired guy he'd gone to school with, looked up when Jace slammed his door. "Well, whadda ya say, Jace?" Rowdy greeted him with a smile.

"Aw, not much, Rowdy. Was just driving by and saw you out here with the car and thought I'd stop. Always liked this car," he said, looking it over.

"That so?" Rowdy said.

Jace nodded. "Truth to tell, always envied you driving this

thing. When I was a kid, kinda wanted to get involved in racing myself. But it wasn't in the cards."

"It's a hell of a lot of fun," Rowdy assured him. "Expensive hobby, no doubt—but I've always had good luck with sponsors, and it works out. Wouldn't trade doing it, that's for sure."

Jace nodded, taking that in. Then lifted his gaze to his old buddy's face. "Tell me if I'm stepping over a line, but any chance you'd ever let me take this around the track once or twice."

Rowdy shrugged. "For an old friend, sure. And if you can handle an eighteen-wheeler, I reckon you can handle this." But then he winked. "Just don't go over fifty." Jace knew these cars exceeded a hundred miles an hour on the track, but couldn't blame Rowdy for wanting a novice to take it slow.

"I'm actually thinking of getting a new one," Rowdy told Jace.

"Why's that?"

Rowdy ran his hand appreciatively along the car's sleek fender. "Aw, you know, it's a toy for grown-ups and guess I'm just ready for a new toy. Gotta sell this one first, though. Know anybody who might be interested?"

THE FOLLOWING AFTERNOON, Shelby biked to Delia's for milk, water, and a few other groceries.

Business at Salty Pete's had been dead, so he'd sent her home early, and told her he'd be closing up for a couple days until the storm passed. "I'll call you when we're back in business," the crusty old man had said. Then pointed a finger in her direction. "Now I know you ain't from around here, so listen to me. You get yourself some groceries in and prepare to be holed up a day or two."

"I heard the storm wouldn't be that bad," she informed him.

His silvery eyebrows shot up. "That's for people with four wheels. You only got two and live in the swamp. Prepare to be holed up. Got it?"

She nodded, and appreciated the advice. "Got it. Thanks."

"Now get outta here," he'd said, waving her away.

She had made only a measly five dollars in tips, but had just cashed a paycheck at the bank in town yesterday, so felt flush with cash—relatively speaking.

Now she thought about what she had at home and what to add to it, given the planning and practicality her shopping currently required. Canned soup—a regular menu item for her lately—would be good for rainy days and could even be heated in a pan in the fireplace if the power went out, so she would add some to her supply. She picked up eggs and a cheap frozen pizza as well, hoping the power would hold—and if not, she had plenty of peanut butter and jelly at home already. Some toilet paper and milk completed her list for today, and collectively, that would be all she could fit in her bicycle basket.

She loaded everything onto the counter and waited as Delia rung it up, making small talk about the storm.

"You need anything when the weather comes, you call me, okay?" Delia said.

Shelby nodded her appreciation. "Thanks. I'm sure I'll be fine, but I'll keep it in mind."

"Ten-fifty-nine," Delia said then.

Which made Shelby study the goods even as Delia began bagging them. She mentally added them up in her head. It didn't seem like enough. It *never* seemed like enough. She hated to look a gift horse in the mouth, but every time she shopped here, she paid less than she expected to.

"Are you sure you're ringing everything up?" she asked Delia, tilting her head slightly.

The other woman blinked. "Yes, of course."

She didn't even double check. Though it was only a handful of items, so maybe she didn't have to.

"It just seems like it should be more."

"The eggs and milk are on sale," Delia said quickly. "Storm discount."

"Oh." She hadn't seen signs to that effect, but...well, who was she to question affordable groceries? "That's nice of you. Most places would *raise* prices at such a time rather than reduce them."

"You take care in the storm, Shelby," Delia told her.

"You, too."

SKIES HAD BEEN SWIRLING with dark clouds all day, and as promised, shortly after dark, Shelby heard the rain begin. She turned on the TV, deciding to watch the storm's progress there—only to find the stations cutting in and out to a point of being unwatchable. Indeed, the antenna hadn't held as the rain sheeted the cottage. She sat in front of the TV for a few minutes anyway, listening to broken bits of a meteorologist's report that—as best she could tell—indicated the bad weather would pass by day after tomorrow, and in Charleston and points southward which included Sassafras, the only result would be heavy rainfall.

Despite the loss of the antenna, she was thankful even just for the voice from the TV when it came, and also glad she'd battened down the hatches in small ways—she'd put her bicycle in the shed, brought in some firewood, and covered the rest with a plastic tarp she'd found in the shed as well.

Leaning back on the couch, she peered over at the bright lights on the Christmas tree and felt grateful.

Grateful to be someplace safe. For even in a tiny cottage under the rains of a tropical storm at the end of a lonely road that ended in a swamp, she felt safe. Safer than she had in Chicago. Safer than she had even a week ago. And that part, she knew, was due to Jace.

Part of her still, on instinct, regretted accepting his kindnesses and worried about where that could lead. But a bigger part of her simply appreciated that he'd come along, and that he'd persisted, and that he'd worked his way past some of her defenses.

She didn't like that he was on her mind. Almost constantly now. It seemed unwise. It felt like attachment.

And yet, he was always there, lingering on the edge of her thoughts.

Or directly in the center of them.

She wasn't sure how she would fill the next two days. She'd quickly become accustomed to the routines of going up the beach to work, or riding her bike into town to Delia's or the library or the diner just past the Rose Tavern—where she'd twice treated herself to a chocolate milkshake because she'd decided it was okay to occasionally squander a couple of dollars on something frivolous if it made her happy. When she wasn't out, she still often worked around the house and yard, making things tidier, bit by bit. She'd started a compost heap in one corner where the yard gave way to woods.

Now she wished she'd invested in a gallon of paint or some other way to start fixing up the *inside*. On the other hand, maybe a rainstorm that kept windows shut wasn't the best time for that. But she still wasn't sure how to fill the time constructively. Without letting bad thoughts or fears sneak in. Those had waned a lot lately. She didn't want to let them get a foothold, and she'd learned that it had a lot to do with keeping busy, both with her mind and her hands.

As she walked to the kitchen to make her dinner, she thought ahead to the rest of the evening. *Maybe I'll read a book. Maybe I'll clean parts of the house I haven't gotten to yet. Maybe I'll make a list of home improvement projects to be tackled as I make more money.*

She opened the old refrigerator—only to hear a sudden *bang, bang, bang* on the front door.

And her heart stopped in her chest.

Had Craig found her?

She froze in place in front of the fridge, too panicked to move.

The pounding continued. *Bang, bang, bang.*

She wanted to run, hide—but where?

Then a voice cut through the sounds of the storm. "Shelby, can you let me in? I'm getting drenched out here!"

Jace.

Her heart resumed beating as she shut the refrigerator and rushed to the door, whisking it open. Standing on her porch holding a soggy pizza box and a six-pack of beer, he looked just as handsome as ever, even dripping from head to toe.

CHAPTER THIRTEEN

*A*s he stepped through the screen door she held open for him, she realized the sideways-blowing rain kept the awning from providing shelter just now.

"What are you doing here?" she asked.

He held up the box. "I'd think this soaking wet pizza would make that obvious."

She lowered her chin, narrowed her gaze. "Ever heard of texting?"

"Storm took out my connection." He cast a small, hopeful smile. "So I had to make a judgment call. I could sit at home alone wondering how you are. Or I could come over. This way, you can just be happy I brought you pizza, and I can be happy I don't have to worry about you. I hope you like pepperoni."

She wanted to kill him.

And she wanted to kiss him.

THEY REHEATED THE PIZZA—WHICH Shelby couldn't deny looked a lot better than her frozen one—under tin foil in the oven, and she got him a towel to dry off with. After popping the tops on two beers, they ate in the living room, taking in the cheerful glow of the Christmas tree, and she confessed how much she'd been enjoying it. Christmas was just over a week away now, and though this would still be the strangest Christmas of her life, the tree was the one thing that reminded her of the season and brought her some joy when she sat near it.

He told her he wanted to put a new lock on her door—claiming the current one was a worn out piece of crap he suspected he could easily push through if he tried. And since she was attempting to learn to accept his help, she said okay. Then informed him of the TV reception problem and he promised to get it fixed as soon as the storm passed. And this time she didn't argue. She just thanked him.

"I hope you don't mind too much that I came over," he said. It was one of the first times she'd ever seen him express self-doubt. "Was it the wrong thing to do? Again?"

She thought it over and admitted the truth. "It wasn't wrong." Despite herself, she was glad he'd come.

"Believe it or not," he said, "I really *am* trying to respect your boundaries. I hate what you've been through and I get your need to be cautious."

"Thank you. For getting that."

He tilted his head. "I just care, that's all. I care and I'm not sure what to do besides show it."

She absorbed that, let it sink down into her heart. *Maybe it's okay to quit being afraid. Maybe it's okay to take this for what it is—kindness. Being controlled, being possessed—that's all behind you. Jace is a good guy—deep down, you know that. He's maybe even...a special guy.*

But wait—don't go there. It's way too soon for that.

127

She had to keep at least *some* walls up for her peace of mind.

Though without quite knowing why, she professed her panicky thoughts when he'd first come to the door. "It was just the way you were pounding—it sounded...angry or something. And so my mind went in the worst possible direction."

"Aw honey—I'm sorry," he said. "It wasn't angry pounding —it was wet pounding. But...I need to pay attention, remember, think about what I'm doing before I do it. Because God knows I don't ever want to make you afraid. I want to do the opposite."

"You do," she admitted. And she almost regretted the words as soon as they left her, but it was too late by the time she cautiously raised her gaze to his.

His voice came low, calm. "I'm glad." And she couldn't deny that there were distinct moments, more and more, when she felt him understanding her particular background and fears, and knowing she needed exactly that: Calm. Quiet. Peace. Assurance.

"Don't go letting that make you think I trust you completely or anything, though," she told him with a playful smile.

He returned it. "Oh, don't worry. If you've made anything clear to me at all, it's that your trust has to be earned."

She nodded succinctly, glad he understood.

Then he flashed a cute look. "But I think I'm doing pretty good so far."

She let out a teasing sigh, rolled her eyes. "One day at a time, Mr. Rose, one day at a time."

"All right, all right—whatever you say, Ms. Scott."

Just then, the meteorologist's voice came from the TV as it blipped to life for a moment, updating them on the storm. Nothing new, more of the same, but being reminded of it made her feel all the more secluded here with him. And the funny thing was—a few days ago the idea of being secluded with him or any other man would have been panic-inducing. But now, with Jace, not so much.

"How was the road?" she asked as the voice on TV mentioned downed power lines and flooding in some areas.

"Good in the four wheel drive. Wouldn't be good in much else, though."

"So that confirms I'm stuck here for a while."

He shrugged, grinned. "Lucky you've got me to keep you company."

She tossed him a glance. "I thought the TV was supposed to alleviate the need for that."

"TV's mostly on the fritz," he reminded her. "Looks like I'm all you've got."

Her heart beat harder now, just from his nearness, just from the sexy look in his eyes. They'd finished their pizza, put their plates aside, and sat at opposite ends of the old couch. Their sock-covered feet touched in the middle, and even just that was enough to have her blood racing.

"True," she heard herself say. Then, "Kiss me."

Totally unplanned. And she'd never initiated a kiss that way before—ever. God knew this was the last time in her life when she'd have expected to suddenly behave so boldly—but maybe everything she'd been through had simply worn down her defenses more than she'd realized. Maybe she was raw. Maybe she was tired. Maybe she was filled with a yearning she couldn't keep pushing down. Maybe she had no choice now but to just stop holding back, just be real, open, vulnerable.

Their eyes met and held for a long moment, so long that she almost began to worry he wasn't going to obey the command. But then she realized he was savoring it, sinking slowly into the moment, into the desire, into the storm.

Slowly he moved toward her, rising up on his knees, then leaning over to place his palms on either side of her on the sofa, slowly encaging her body with his. But this cage felt good. Not scary. Not like he was stealing her control. But more like she *wanted* that—just in this moment. She wanted him to take her, guide her, bend her to his will sexually. She wanted him to lead, touch, enter, grasp, make her moan, make her scream.

It was an animal instinct, this sort of submission—but one she'd never expected to experience again. And already, here it was, pummeling her like the rain on the roof, swallowing her like a deluge.

His kiss was slow, deep, demanding. She closed her eyes, lifted her fingertips to his stubbled jaw, let herself sink there, into the kiss, into the unexpected surrender.

And everything after that was easy. It was easy to let him take her clothes off, easy to watch with heat in her veins as he sheathed himself, easy to part her legs for him, easy to let him slide his way deep inside her.

She never held in a whimper or a moan. When he kissed her, she kissed him back, hard. She let her arms twine around his neck, gripped his thick hair in her fists—she wrapped her legs around his hips, as well, meeting each thrust, pulling him tight against her, again, again.

"I want to make you come so hard, honey," he rasped in her ear. "I want you to ride me—ride me until you explode."

Heat rose to her cheeks—and also to the crux of her thighs, even more than it had already. This wasn't her usual mode of sex—with Craig, with anyone. And yet—tonight, in this newly recognized state of rawness, she realized his words had only heightened her excitement. "Let me on top of you," she heard herself murmur, breath labored.

And together they rolled their bodies until their positions had switched and she straddled him naked on the couch. And certainly it wasn't the first time she'd done this—it wasn't even the first time with Jace—but it felt new. It came with a new abandon, a new freedom. She ground the softest, most sensitive part of her on that oh-so-hard and rigid part of him, soaking up the pleasure, pressing deeper into it, letting it begin to drown her. She gave herself over to her body's urges and instincts as never before—letting herself feel as wild and untamed as the swamp that circled the cottage, as the storm that beat at the door—and when she toppled head-long into orgasm, it thundered through her with a power she'd never experienced. She screamed out as the waves of pleasure shook her again and again.

"Oh God, honey," he growled below her, clearly moved and excited by her climax. So excited that, "Aw, I can't stop —I'm coming, too." He thrust up into her so powerfully that it lifted her weight from atop him and left her with the sensation that she'd never been so physically connected to a man.

She collapsed gently on his chest, spent, the only sound that of the rain blanketing the house. And she nestled warmly against him feeling, indeed, safe.

JACE AWOKE HOLDING HER. She smelled sweet—some fruity scent, likely from a shampoo or soap. Tropical storms weren't good for much, but they were damn good for this. Ever since taking over the nursery, he spent a lot of time feeling like he was supposed to be somewhere he wasn't, like there was a never-ending list of things to do or people waiting on him—it was a constant responsibility he hadn't gotten quite used to yet. But right now, he had no place else to be but here.

When she stirred against him, he peered down to see her

lift her sleepy head from his chest and gave her a small smile. "That was…intense."

She bit her lip, looked just a little bit sheepish. He liked it. Most of the women he slept with didn't have a sheepish bone in their willing bodies. But Shelby's eyes right now told him this wasn't everyday sex for her. And what guy didn't get off on that a little? "Yeah," she whispered.

He glanced toward the ceiling. "Doesn't sound like the rain is letting up anytime soon."

She shook her head. "Nope."

"I can head home if you want…or I could also stay."

She bit her lip, looking tempted. He liked that, too. "What if there's flooding? What if you can't leave in the morning?"

He shrugged. "Got no particular place to go."

She tilted her head. "No Christmas trees to sell?"

It made him let out a light laugh. "Anybody out buying Christmas trees in this weather needs to have their heads examined. And besides, if there are any big Christmas tree emergencies, I have employees who can handle it."

He thought she looked pleased by his answer. "Well then, guess there's no reason for you to go back out into the storm."

And damn if *her* answer hadn't left *him* happy as well. More than he could even fathom. Because yeah, sure, he'd come here with pizza and a mind to stay over if she'd let him. But also with the notion that if she didn't, it was no big deal. And now…well, staying with her tonight somehow sounded better than he'd even thought it could when he'd impulsively headed out in the rain, grabbing the last pizza that the local pizza parlor would consent to make before they, too, closed up for the storm.

"Getting chilly," he told her, and though they had again pulled down the small quilt from the back of the sofa, he eased out from under her beautifully naked form to build a fire in the hearth.

Then he curled back up with her in the glow of the tree and the flames, and they talked. About everything.

He told her about stopping by Rowdy's, explaining a little about different kinds of race cars, that his particular passion was dirt track racing, that Rowdy was going to take him to a track upstate in a few days when they both had the time and give him some lessons, let him see how it felt to be behind the wheel. "I'm glad you suggested I look into this. I mean, I could have stopped and talked to Rowdy any time, but I'd just never thought about it. And you made me think about it. And who knows—may not lead anywhere—but even just getting to take the car around the oval sounds damn fun. So thank you." He added a kiss.

She told him more about her life before the bastard Craig, and he liked hearing who she'd been before that. Up to now, all he'd really gleaned was that she was a woman on the run from something. But as they lay cuddling in the firelight, the scent of pine making the room even cozier, he learned that she'd once been the editor of her high school yearbook, and she'd played the flute in the pep band. She'd enjoyed her short career in advertising and missed being creative but planned to find other ways to do that soon, and hoped someday to maybe get back into that line of work. She loved mystery novels, and dogs, and chocolate cake, and Halloween parties.

"But Christmas was always my favorite holiday up until Mom died," she told him. "It wasn't the same after that—for lots of reasons." Then she smiled, thinking back. "We had lots of little traditions, just the two of us."

"Like what?" he asked.

She met his gaze. "We used to make French toast with extra powdered sugar on Christmas morning. She called it snow toast when I was little. And there was no opening presents until we'd eaten our snow toast listening to the Elvis Christmas album which—now that I think about it—she probably listened to in this very house growing up."

He smiled back. "That sounds nice, honey."

"We used to go to the Festival of Trees in Indy, and the Christmas Parade in Noblesville, rain or shine. We would make cookies and give them to people at places like the dry cleaners or the post office—just to brighten up their holidays and make them feel appreciated."

He shot her a look. "And you gave me such a hard time about brightening up *your* holidays." Then let his expression soften. "I hope they get brighter again. I mean, I hope someday you can really love Christmas again like you used to."

She didn't reply to that directly, but instead told him, "Your mom's cookies were really good, by the way."

He grinned. "I know. And we Roses don't share them with just anybody, so you should feel honored."

She laughed. "I know homemade cut-out cookies take a lot of time and effort, so I appreciate you sharing." Then she asked him, "Who did you tell her they were for?"

"Same person I told her the ornaments were for. A friend." He winked.

And she lowered her chin onto his chest. "I guess you left out the 'with benefits' part."

Now it was he who laughed. "Yeah—don't think she'd want to know that. Though…"

"What?"

He shook his head, regretting what he'd almost said. "Nothing."

"Tell me."

"No."

"Yes. You can't start to say something and then stop like that. It's not fair."

He flashed her a look of challenge. "What if I know you wouldn't like what I was gonna say?"

She pursed her lips, appeared stern. "Say it anyway and I won't hold it against you."

"Okay. Here goes. Ready?"

"Ready."

"I wish you wanted to be more than friends with benefits."

Another sigh from the pretty girl snuggling naked with him. "For your information," she said, "I don't *want* to be friends with benefits. I've *never* wanted that, ever. It's not really who I am. I just…don't know *how* to be right now."

He understood that. He hated it, hated what that asshole had done to her—but he understood it. "How about being… open to possibilities?" he suggested. "Open to…me?"

She blinked prettily, clearly thinking that over, and let out a sigh. "I guess…I can give that a try."

THE NEXT MORNING they made French toast in a skillet—him in his boxer briefs, her in his T-shirt—minus the powdered sugar because she didn't have any. Rain still engulfed the house, and when Jace suggested they go back to bed, grabbing her wrist and pulling her in that direction, she didn't argue. Oh yeah, tropical storms were starting to hold a whole new appeal.

As he lay her back in her bed, he glanced up to see some of her beribboned mistletoe hanging in the window, so on impulse, he reached over and lifted the red ribbon off the old-fashioned window lock and drew it down.

"What are you doing?" she asked with a suspicious grin.

He spoke low, deep. "Just using this as the Christmas gods intended."

And with that, he held it over both their heads, then leaned down to kiss her, long and warm and delicious.

"Mmm," she purred. "You might just make me start liking Christmas again, Mr. Rose."

"Well, there's more where that came from, Ms. Scott," he informed her—and then, propped on his elbow at her side and still holding the mistletoe aloft by its ribbon, he moved it down her body, using his free hand to push up the loose tee she wore and then letting it hover over her beautiful, bare, coral-tipped breasts. After which he bent to kiss first one, then the other, soon laving and licking and suckling, forcing from her hot sighs and whimpers that made him even harder than he already was.

From there, he eased the dangling ball of white berries down over her pale stomach, kissing his way from her breasts to her waist. A quick glance up at her face revealed that she bit her lip as she watched him, eyes half shut, expression one of sweet surrender. Damn, she turned him on. Even just lying there, letting him make her feel good. Because everything had changed. He was unraveling the mysteries.

And even now, he wanted more of her. Proving that this wasn't *about* mysteries. Mysteries had made him want in her door. Everything else about her made him want to stay.

He shifted the mistletoe further down her body, letting it guide his kisses past her navel and onto the mound of tidy pale brown hair below. Letting out a sexy little breath that heightened his desire, she parted her legs, welcoming his kisses even lower. He gave her another quick glance, their gazes connecting with heat, as he moved the ball of mistletoe over the sweet spot where she was moist and open for him.

Another kiss, directly where he knew she would feel it most, drew from her a quick, hot breath, followed by a low moan. A moan that told him she wanted more. And he was happy to deliver.

Abandoning the mistletoe because he needed his hands as well as his mouth to pleasure her, he licked deeply between her legs, gratified with the whimper that left her at each stroke of his tongue. She lifted her lips to meet his ministrations, soon moving rhythmically against his mouth. The taste and scent of her enveloped him until they were all he knew.

Making a woman come had always excited Jace, but when Shelby came for him it went beyond anything he'd experienced. And when she climaxed now, against his mouth, crying out her pleasure against the backdrop of the unending rain battering the windows, it made him need to be inside her more than he needed to breathe.

Rising up over her, he used his hands to spread her legs farther, then drove his aching erection into her warmly sheathing flesh. A deep groan echoed from her soft lips, and then they were moving together, rocking together, in a perfect, timeless rhythm.

Beneath him, Shelby lost herself to the way Jace's deep plunges echoed to the tips of her fingers and toes. She lost herself to the closeness, to the pleasure, to that same raw openness she'd experienced with him last night. She followed every instinct and urge, released every response that rose within her.

She'd left Chicago to be free—free of fear and free to be in control of her own life. But the freedom she felt with Jace went beyond that. With him she was free to be her most sensual self, her most feminine self. And yes, maybe it somehow came with simply being weary of putting up protective walls. But it was also something he brought out in her. Her intense attraction to him combined with the care he'd shown for her was the perfect combination to open up her most authentic self, a part of her she'd never even known was hiding inside.

Afterward, they lay quietly together just listening to the storm. It was white noise at this point, but made her feel all the more cocooned with him. She rolled over to peer at him in the dim daylight filtering in the windows. "You should feel special," she told him.

He met her gaze. "Why's that?"

She wasn't sure why she was confessing this, especially as hard as she'd worked to tell him as little as possible up until recently—but maybe she just wanted him to know. "Because I never expected to feel this way. What I mean is...I don't think I've ever let myself go this much with a man. In bed." For some reason she blushed, though.

Which made him grin. "You should feel special, too," he told her, "because...I'm not usually like this with women."

"Like what?"

"Like...worried about them, wanting to make sure they're safe. I probably seem like some knight in shining armor type, but I'm not. Only with you."

"Your other friends with benefits don't get bicycles and firewood?"

He laughed. "Afraid not. I mean, sure, if they *asked* me for bicycles and firewood, I'd be happy to help—but I don't usually go around foisting my bikes on people."

She smiled. "Why me?"

He shifted his head on the pillow, looking deliciously handsome. "I'm not sure. You just...mystified me. Made me want to uncover the mystery, see what made you tick. And now that I know, I admire the hell out of you for being so damn brave. Never complaining, never asking for help—just starting over like this. But like it or not, it makes me want to take care of you. And I know you don't want that."

She drew in a breath, felt the need to clarify. "It's just that...I need to know I can take care of *myself*."

"I get that. But there's one problem with it."

"Which is?"

"I think I'm falling in love with you," he said. "And what sort of guy falls in love with a girl without wanting to take care of her and make sure she's okay?"

Shelby blinked. "Wait. What did you just say?"

He closed his eyes for a second, looked regretful. "Shit. I blew it, didn't I? I've freaked you out." He shook his head. "I just...said what I felt, and now you're gonna worry I'm moving too fast and trying to make it something you're not comfortable with."

Next to him, she took another deep breath, tried to think this through. And she knew she should stop, be more careful, end this madness—this madness that was the exact opposite of what she'd wanted when she'd come here. And yet she heard herself spilling out still more unguarded honesty. "All of that is true," she said. "You *are* moving too fast and making it something I'm not comfortable with. So I should tell you to leave now, and make you stay away, and not want anything more to do with you. I should call a halt to this whole thing. But there's one problem with *that*."

"What is it?" he asked.

"I'm falling in love with you, too."

CHAPTER FOURTEEN

"*T*hat, honey," he said, "is the best news I've heard in…maybe my whole damn life."

Her breath trembled now, though. "Is it? Because…this isn't what I planned. And it scares me."

He rolled closer to her in bed, lifted his hands to her face. "I know. And I get why. But I promise it's okay. It's more than okay. It's…amazing is what it is. I mean, I wasn't looking for this, either. I was just coasting along, trying to get used to the daily grind of the nursery and feeling a little stuck in this town, and then…you. And I don't feel stuck anymore, Shelby. I feel…like I'm exactly where I'm supposed to be." He leaned over, kissed her. "Trust in that. Trust in *me*."

SHE SPENT the rest of that day and night learning to trust. Because they'd both crossed this line, wittingly or not, and she'd meant what she said—she'd fallen in love with the sweet, pushy, handsome jerk who'd shoved his way into her life. And despite logic and caution and everything she'd told herself about why this couldn't happen, she already couldn't imagine her life here without him. He made everything better. That simple. He made *her* better.

The day was filled with grilled cheese and soup for lunch, and reheated pizza for dinner. It was filled with more talking: places they'd been or wanted to go, childhood memories, stories about family and friends. She showed him picture albums from her girlhood—showed him her mother, showed him her life. Her *real* life before everything had gone crazy.

He wanted her to come to his family's Christmas celebration. And that sounded scary and fast and, again, so different than what she'd expected. And yet—it was Christmas. And maybe, just maybe, she should let him make Christmas special for her again. She thought if anyone could, it was Jason Rose.

After dark, the rain stopped. According to the voices on TV, the storm had begun to dissipate and what remained was moving up the coast and then back out to sea. All that was left in Sassafras was the drying out. "No major damage reported," a female anchorperson said, "so Santa can come to South Carolina on schedule as we say bah, humbug to Tropical Storm Terri and send her on her way."

Jace spent the night again, and by morning they were both happily exhausted from sex. "I never thought I'd say this, but I could go for some more rain," he told her, lying with her under the covers.

She glanced out the window where the view was clear for the first time since the storm had made landfall. "I guess since it's over, you need to get back to real life."

He nodded. "Yeah—back to the daily grind. But…I'll have more to smile about now, after the last couple days." Every kiss from Jace took away any lingering doubts and fears, and the one he delivered now was no different. "I need to head to the nursery, make sure everything's okay there, and get the tree business rolling again for folks who wait 'til the last minute." Christmas was less than a week away now.

"But I'll call you, let you know how the road looks. And… honey, please let me loan you the spare car. Okay?"

She held firm. "Believe it or not, I've really come to like the bike."

"Well, you can keep the bike, too," he told her playfully. "Ride it as much as you like. But I'll feel better if you have a car and can get around easier when that's more convenient."

She responded with a long sigh. "I guess it *would* be nice to be able to buy more than a few items of groceries at a time." She tilted her head on the pillow. "Tell you what—I'll think about it. Maybe after Christmas. How's that?"

He smiled, kissed her forehead. "That's good. If you'll take the car that would be a nice Christmas present for me."

Standing at the door in a T-shirt a little while later, sending him out into the mushy yard to his truck, a certain wistfulness stole over her to know this magical couple of days had ended. But another emotion buffeted her, too—the almost shocking feeling that…she could relax. *Really* relax. Because she was in love with a wonderful man and life was getting more beautiful by the day, far faster than she'd imagined possible.

"ALL RIGHT, Mrs. Weathers, you enjoy that tree and have a merry Christmas. Tom'll get it tied on to your roof. And if you and your husband have any trouble getting it inside, just give us a call and we'll send somebody over to help."

Jace watched another happy customer go, surprised at how brisk business had been. Quite a few locals *had* put off their decorating until after the storm. They all seemed relieved to find trees still available and it left him feeling good to provide them. Maybe running the nursery could be a little more satisfying than he'd let him himself believe up to now.

And it didn't hurt that he'd had a talk with his parents this morning—when they'd stopped by to remind him he still hadn't added lights to the trees out front. He'd told them—with love—that he had to run the place his way, and that they had to accept that. It was a discussion he should have had without waiting this long, but he supposed the last couple days with Shelby had inspired him. Fortunately, they'd seemed to understand and take it well—the nursery was his now, at their bequest, and it was time for them to let it go. It had been a good talk.

"What the hell are you grinning about?"

He looked up to see Rick, and behind him Tanner, who had just walked in. "I haven't seen you look this happy since before you sold your rig," Tanner observed.

Jace knew what he was happy about, of course. It wasn't the nursery business or the end of the storm or Christmas so much as it was the new woman in his life. And he didn't see much reason to hide it from his brothers, who were also his best friends. "Met a girl," he said simply.

His brothers exchanged glances. And Tanner said, "You meet lots of girls. Doesn't usually set you to walking around smiling like a fool."

Jace just laughed. "Well, guess this one's special."

Again, Rick and Tanner looked at each other, clearly puzzled. And Jace supposed he understood why—for all the women he'd dated over the years, he wasn't sure he'd ever described one as special. He was the king of the casual relationship and not getting too serious. He'd had a whole country to see, after all, and he'd never wanted to be tied down. But funny how quick things could change. And hell, he had a feeling he'd be head over heels for Shelby regardless of that, but the fact that he no longer traveled for long stretches to make a living sort of made the situation seem almost...fated.

"Special how?" Rick asked, brow knit with confusion.

Jace tried to think how to explain in a way his brother would understand. "Special like Mia is to you, I guess."

One more exchange of glances between his siblings—before Tanner said, "Who are you and what have you done with our brother?"

It made him let out another laugh. "Look, it had to happen eventually, right?" Both Rick and Tanner had always been more prone to having relationships, getting serious with girls at least on occasion. Jace hadn't until now, but the time had officially come.

"Well, who *is* this girl?" Rick asked.

Jace leaned over, resting his elbows on the counter next to the cash register. "The one I mentioned to you a couple weeks ago."

Rick's eyebrows shot up. "The crazy, down-on-her-luck one?"

"I never called her crazy," Jace was quick to point out. "Just mysterious."

"And I said she sounded like trouble," Rick reminded him, his big brother tendencies coming through in his voice.

But Jace was used to that. "Yeah, yeah, I remember. But she's *not* trouble. She just had to *get away* from some trouble, that's all."

Rick sent him a sideways glance. "That still sounds like trouble."

"What was the mystery?" Tanner asked.

"A guy who was bad to her. It's her business, so I'll leave it at that, but she's been through a lot and just wants to put it behind her."

"I still don't like it," Rick groused.

"You don't like your brother being happy?" Jace gave his head a persuasive tilt. "Come on, man—how about a little support?"

Despite always thinking he knew best, his older brother let out a sigh of concession. "Okay, I guess you're right. If this chick makes you happy, I'll give her a chance."

Jace smiled. "Good—because I'm bringing her to Mom and Dad's for Christmas."

Once more, Rick and Tanner exchanged looks, Tanner muttering, "Who *is* this guy?"

WHEN SHELBY GOT a text saying Salty Pete's was back open for business and she'd be expected for her eleven o'clock shift, she found herself downright excited to get ready for work. She'd actually missed seeing Pete and Lonna and Reggie, and even looked forward to waiting on customers.

One more surprise in her new world—being a hermit wasn't as easy as she'd thought. Or maybe Jace had just convinced her she didn't have to be afraid of everyone, that it was okay to live a normal life. And she was beginning to *feel* almost normal. Craig had messed with her head until she hadn't known which end was up—but she was starting to see clearly again. As clear as the blue sky when she emerged from the swamp path onto the beach on her walk to work.

The storm clouds had faded completely overnight, leaving behind a bright, cheerful blue sky. Up north, a day like this wasn't exactly common at Christmastime, but it was just another part of her new normal—a normal that was beginning to seem pretty damn good.

Mostly it was thanks to Jace—no denying that. Without him, she'd just be eking by, living day to day, not knowing what tomorrow held. *With* him came a sense of hope and promise and…again, safety. He'd made her risky new life more bearable from the start, whether she'd wanted to let him or not. And now, he'd filled it with the last thing she'd expected: love.

She still couldn't believe she'd let herself fall for him. But her mother had always said you don't choose who you love; love chooses you. And as she walked up the thin, barren beach, the brown sand packed tight after the rain, she couldn't believe the utter happiness that flowed through her veins.

"You survive the storm okay, girlie?" Pete asked when she walked in, the open air building's rain tarps lifted and the place looking none the worse for wear. As usual, he didn't smile and spoke gruffly.

"Just fine," she pleasantly replied. "And you?"

"Always have, always will."

The lunch crowd was heavier than any since she'd started waiting tables—clearly low country folk missed their seafood during a storm, even when it was almost Christmas. But she handled the rush well, feeling skilled and secretly thankful she'd had a couple of weeks' training before this.

When it died down and the place was mostly empty again, Pete said with his usual dour expression, "You done good there, Shelby girl."

"Thanks." She hadn't counted her tips yet, but had probably already made twice as much as any other day before.

"Had my doubts when you first showed up here, but reckon I'm glad Jace talked me into hiring you."

As the words struck home, Shelby's back went rigid and she blinked. "What?"

Pete answered as if she were hard of hearing instead of just confused and taken aback. "*Said I had my doubts about you, but glad Jace talked me into giving you a chance.*"

Well, at least this confirmed that she hadn't misunderstood him. "Jace asked you to hire me?"

The old man nodded, clearly not catching on that she was thrown by the news. "Vouched for ya and said he'd take it as a personal favor. I've told ya before I feel obliged to return favors, and the Roses have done enough for me."

She drew in her breath. "So you wouldn't have hired me if Jace hadn't asked?"

At this, Pete tilted his head first one way, then the other, obviously thinking it over. "Nothing personal, but probably not. You were carrying a garden tool and looked like you'd just wandered in from the beach."

Which was exactly what she'd done, of course. But it was shocking—and disturbing—to discover Jace had gotten the job for her. And let her think otherwise. All this time.

"You oughta thank him," Pete said, "'cause it's worked out good."

She tried to force a smile. *Oh, I'll thank him, all right.*

A knot stayed in her stomach the rest of the day. Because this changed things. Jace hadn't been honest with her. And even if he was just trying to help...well, she'd made it very clear that she needed to do things on her own. And that she required truthfulness from him.

She'd been so happy—giddy happy, silly happy—but this felt like a kick in the gut.

It was with a much more troubled heart that she later rode her bike to Delia's for a few groceries she needed after the storm. Jace had let her know earlier that the road was fine other than some puddles, which she wove through as she made her way to the market.

She picked up milk, OJ, bread, some frozen fish filets, and instant macaroni and cheese. She made the usual small talk as Delia rung up her order—they'd both come through the heavy rains just fine, it had been a light storm compared to many Delia had seen, and the market would be closed on Christmas Eve and Christmas Day.

When, as always, the total for the order seemed impossibly low, Shelby asked her, "Are you sure? I know it seems crazy that I keep questioning this, but it just doesn't seem like enough."

"It is," Delia assured her—although, in Shelby's opinion—too quickly to have even considered the question.

And then, also as always, Delia tore the receipt off the top of the cash register, wadded it up, and tossed it in a trashcan behind the counter. It had never struck Shelby until just now that Delia never gave her the receipt—at first claiming low ink and then later just throwing them away. It had seemed like perhaps a small town quirk that she would assume Shelby didn't want it. But now she said, "Can I see the receipt?"

Delia hesitated—and Shelby wondered just what the heck was going on here.

Then Delia slowly reached down to extract it from the wastebasket, saying, "Yeah, sure," but sounding wholly uneasy.

She handed the receipt over just as guardedly, looking troubled, and leaving Shelby all the more perplexed. Shelby straightened the receipt in her hands and studied it. And felt all the more confused as she said, "You didn't ring up the orange juice, and you only charged me a dollar apiece for the milk and fish, which isn't even close to right." She raised her gaze to the other woman. "What's going on?"

Now Delia, usually the picture of easy-going confidence, appeared flustered, guilty, and at a loss for words.

"Delia," Shelby pleaded in frustration. "Come on. What's the big secret here?"

Finally the other woman blew out a breath and said under her breath, "Jace is going to kill me."

"What?"

Delia's eyes dropped nervously to the counter. "Jace... gave me money to cover some of your groceries. Just a little. He didn't want you to know."

Shelby's outrage must have shown in her eyes because Delia was quick to go on.

"He was just being a good guy, worried for you while you get on your feet. It was really sweet if you think about it—it came from a good place."

Shelby pursed her lips, trying to wrap her mind around this. Every time she'd come here, her order had been subsidized by Jace. Every single time. She felt like an idiot in front of Delia. And a pauper to boot. She didn't care if it came from a good place—he'd made her feel foolish and embarrassed.

She could see that Delia was embarrassed, too, having colluded and kept it from her. And she supposed the other woman had only been doing what an old friend had asked and maybe it had seemed harmless. But it also made what Shelby had thought was a burgeoning friendship feel a little less authentic than it had before, so she just steeled herself and said, "Thank you. For telling me the truth. From now on, I'll be paying full price, the same as every other customer, and meanwhile I'll settle this with Jace."

She picked up her bags and walked out the door, loaded them into her bike's basket, then headed for home, her heart pounding so hard it hurt.

How dare him! How dare he go behind her back this way. It was bad enough that he'd gotten her a job and never even told her about it—but to pay for her groceries? Without her consent? In a sneaky way?

She knew what it was to be manipulated and this fit the bill. He'd forced her to accept something without a choice, making her dependent on him without her even knowing it, making it so she wasn't taking care of herself at all, building in her a false sense of security. It felt all too familiar—because she'd been down this road before. Her stomach churned with memories of Craig secretly paying her bills—and that while it had lifted one burden it had created another by leaving her beholden to him. She'd never really had the choice—she'd just been swept along into obligation and commitment by virtue of his pushy actions, all disguised as…kindness.

Kindness.

Like she'd thought Jace had shown her.

She thought of that word over and over in relation to him —but now it seemed…false. Forced. It made her feel weak. Confused. Like she didn't really know him. Like he wasn't who she thought. Like this could turn into one more disaster.

That's what you get for relaxing. That's what you get for letting someone into your life. That's what you get for falling in love.

Her mother's voice echoed in her ear. *You don't find love— it finds you.*

So what do I do now, Mom?

She fought back tears as she turned onto Cypress Stump Road, heading for home—and then, damn it, she rounded a bend half a mile from the cottage only to see an alligator in the road, sunning itself on this bright but suddenly unsettling afternoon. And it wasn't a little one, either. Probably five or six feet long.

Her first thought: *What would Jace tell me to do?* It made sense to wonder—he'd grown up here and knew the practical answers to such things.

But she banished the thought immediately—who gave a damn what Jace would say? She could take care of herself and she would! She was a capable woman who didn't need a man, who didn't need *anyone*, and who wasn't going to let a stupid alligator make her day any worse than it already was.

So she kept pedaling. Right toward it. She'd ride right past it.

Even if it started looking a lot bigger stretched across the road as she got nearer.

Even if her heart rose to her throat as it suddenly hit her that she had no idea if this was dangerous, if she was being an idiot, if she should pedal fast or slow, if she might suddenly end up dead or mangled. But if so, at least she'd go down on her own terms.

She pedaled fast. On instinct.

She decided to go by on the side where its tail was rather than its head and hoped that made sense.

It lifted its scaly, prehistoric head and turned dark, emotionless eyes on her—as she went zipping past at the top speed the bike would go, and she only started breathing again when she realized she'd made it and the alligator seemed unfazed.

Then she found herself panting, shaken, struggling to keep pedaling—but no way was she going to stop now. She needed to put some more distance between her and that ugly gator.

As she rounded the last curve that brought the cottage into view, she thought she'd had about all she could take today. But apparently she'd have to deal with a little more—because Jace's truck was parked outside and the door to her house was standing wide open.

He apparently thought it was okay to let himself in. Well, he was about to be set straight on that.

Leaning the bike against the porch, she lifted her bags from the basket, then looked up see him standing in the doorway. Smiling.

Damn it, that smile melted her heart.

But she didn't let it melt her resolve.

"What the hell do you think you're doing?" she confronted him.

He appeared equally as unfazed as the alligator. "I just remounted your antenna. Though I'll still get Tanner over here to take a look—make sure it's sturdy enough for wind and rain. And I'm about to install a new lock on your door. I was right, honey—all I had to do to get in was turn the knob."

Storming past him, she plopped her bags on the kitchen table, then emerged back into the living room to say, "You are unbelievable."

He looked nonplused. "Huh?"

She hardly knew where to begin. The job? The groceries? Thinking it was okay to just come into her house when she wasn't home? She blew out a breath, and cut right to the heart of the matter. "This was a bad idea."

"What was a bad idea?"

"All of this. Me and you. Thinking I could trust you. Thinking you understood my boundaries. It was a huge mistake."

He stood before her, a screwdriver in one hand and a lock mechanism in the other. "What's wrong? What are you talking about?"

"What am I talking about?" She looked him straight in the sexy blue eyes and knew she had to be strong, not be taken in or seduced by everything she loved about him. "I'm talking about the job you got for me! I'm talking about the groceries you paid for behind my back! I'm talking about this"—she motioned to the stuff in his hands—"thinking you can just come in here and start changing things when I'm not even here!"

"Honey, I—"

"Don't honey me! You had no right, Jace. I trusted you. Because you made me believe I could. And yet you've done things behind my back that make me feel weak and helpless

—and lied to. You've made me accept help without my consent. You did things that...that *he* would do!"

The last part made him flinch. "Whoa. Wait a minute. You're comparing me to *him*? The bastard who locked you in a condo? Who quit your job for you? Who knocks his girlfriends off balconies and down stairs?"

Okay, it sounded harsh when he put it *that* way. But she had to stand her ground here. She'd gotten in this mess by *not* standing her ground. With Craig. And then with Jace. She had no choice. She couldn't keep letting men push her around and run her life and think it was okay.

"Well, maybe I've had enough of men who interfere with my jobs! And the locks on my doors!"

She could almost see the lightbulb go on over his head—realizing he'd actually been tampering with the same parts of her life Craig once had. But he still looked just as offended. "I got you a job—not took one from you!" he pointed out. "And I wanted you to be able to lock people out, not be locked in—big difference. I do things to help you, not hurt you."

"Still, how am I am to know?" she spewed at him desperately. "How am I to know you *aren't* like that? He seemed nice in the beginning, too! I think you keep forgetting that part. He seemed...as great as you do. And then I found out the hard way that it was all a charade. And I lost everything. *Everything.* How the hell do you expect me to take that kind of chance again? How can you not understand that every time you give me unwanted help that it just makes me feel beholden to you, dependent on you, and that that's exactly what *he* did?"

"Well, in fairness to me, I didn't know about Craig until a few days ago. And I've been trying to honor your boundaries —but I guess I thought when we said we loved each other, that changed things."

He sounded almost angry about that—and maybe she

could see his point. They *had* professed love for each other. But that was one more mistake on her part because clearly she wasn't ready for love if this was what it entailed. And she was still absorbing the things he hadn't told her.

"But when you found out about him...well, did it ever occur to you that maybe you should come clean with me about the groceries?"

He shook his head. "No, actually. It didn't even cross my mind—I'd forgotten about it. Guess I didn't think it was that big a deal."

"Maybe that's the problem. You don't think *any* of this is a big deal. And to me, it's *all* a big deal. Because this little bit of a life I'm carving out here is all I have. That's it. There's nothing else. No family, no friends, no money, and no belongings. I'm alone in the world, Jace."

He took a step toward her. "You're not alone anymore, honey. You have me."

She cringed then, tears gathering behind her eyes. Because she wanted him, so very badly, but..."No, I don't. I can't be with someone I can't trust, someone who thinks they know better than me, someone who does things behind my back. How could I *ever* want to be with someone like that, given what I just got away from?" She stopped, shook her head, then spoke more quietly. "I was just getting brave enough to trust, Jace—and you ruined that. In so many ways. I can't have that in my life. I can't have *you* in my life."

CHAPTER FIFTEEN

*J*ace stood before her, frozen and disbelieving. Part of him wanted to argue, plead his case. Another part of him even understood—with sudden clarity—where she was coming from. Despite his best intentions, maybe he hadn't realized—despite his best efforts—exactly *how* fragile she was. Maybe he'd tried to make everything be okay for her too fast because he wanted it that way.

But the biggest thing he knew right now was that she wanted him gone. And that it didn't really matter who was right or who was wrong. It didn't matter that he'd only wanted to look out for her and keep her safe and make her life better. It didn't matter that he'd thought they were on the same page now and that things would get easier with her. It only mattered that, besides no longer trusting him now, she'd actually had the nerve to compare him to Craig.

That stung deep. And was the sole thing that made him walk out the door. "You don't want me in your life? Fine, I won't be in your life." He tossed the screwdriver he held into his toolbox, closed it, and left.

A lump rose to his throat as he took the steps toward his truck, dropped the toolbox in the bed, and got inside. It was all he could do not to look back, not to worry for her already, not to keep trying to make things right. But that damn comparison to an asshole lunatic kept him moving.

Maybe he'd made mistakes. Maybe even big ones. But he'd never, ever hurt her or any other woman willingly. His mistakes had come from how damn much he cared for her—how much he'd cared almost from the very start—and if she couldn't see that, the hell with her.

Starting the truck, he pressed on the gas and headed back down Cypress Stump Road for the last time.

Tinsel glittered in the dim light of the Rose Tavern, Madonna sang "Santa Baby" over the sound system, and Jace drowned his sorrows in an extremely alcoholic lime green concoction his brother had thought up called a Screaming Grinch. And that sure as hell fit his mood. All around him, other people were drinking holiday toasts and having Christmas gatherings, a few even opening gifts—but Jace couldn't have given a damn less about the fact that Christmas was a few days away.

"Gimme another Grinch," he said, draining the martini glass it had come in.

Behind the bar, Rick looked from him to Mia, who sat on a stool next to Jace. "Gonna have to drive him home for me if I do."

She nodded. "Against my better judgment of being a party to this, okay."

Rick only sighed. "He's a big boy. So another Screaming Grinch, coming up."

He'd told them both, and Tanner as well, what had

happened. His younger brother had walked to the other end of the bar to say hello to some friends, but now he came back, taking the stool on the other side of Jace.

"I say good riddance," Rick said as he mixed the drink. "I knew that chick was bad news."

"I liked her," Mia countered, referring to the day Shelby had delivered lunch from Salty Pete's. "I'm really sorry things didn't last. It sounds like she's just got some big things to work through."

Jace spoke grimly. "She didn't want me around from the start and I should have paid attention to her then."

"Well, at least it was quick," Tanner said. "Like ripping off a bandaid. They say it takes half as long to get over somebody as the time you were with them. So you should get over her fast, right?"

Jace just looked at him. His little brother meant well. But he had no idea what the hell he was talking about. "I never felt this way about a woman before. I don't think it'll be quick. I think my life is gonna suck for a while, maybe forever—that's what I think."

Just then, Rowdy Cutler wandered up. "Jace buddy, that you?"

Jace looked over his shoulder. He was in no mood to be cordial, but tried—even if it came out sounding rough. "Rowdy. Hey."

His old friend laughed. "Damn—I'm off work the rest of the week for the holiday—was gonna ask if you want to run up to Sumter tomorrow, do some laps and see how you like the car. But maybe another time would be better."

Jace supposed his drunkenness must show. And hell, he'd been looking forward to this—but just now, it was hard to be excited about *anything*. "Yeah, probably. But thanks anyway."

"What's he talking about?" Rick asked from the other side of the bar.

Rowdy answered for Jace, explaining. "I'm in the market for a new race car and your brother expressed interest in taking the old one for a...test drive, guess you might say."

Both his siblings looked surprised until Jace reminded them, "You guys know I always wanted to drive one." He shook his head. "I don't know—figured it might not be too late for an old dog to learn a new trick. But hell, probably just wishful thinking."

"I think it sounds like a damn good idea," Rick said, catching him off-guard. Then to Rowdy, "Tomorrow's fine."

Jace lifted his head, widened his eyes, doubtful. "It is?"

Rick gave a sharp, short nod. "Yep, and I'll come along, too, if it's okay with Rowdy."

"More the merrier as far as I'm concerned," Rowdy said.

"Hell, I already let the crew off for Christmas," Tanner added, "so I'll make it four."

"Sounds like a plan—but first things first," Rick said, looking to Jace. "Need to mix up my best hangover prevention recipe for *you*. And for *you*—" He looked to Tanner, then placed the newly made electric green drink on the bar and shoved it in his direction. "One Screaming Grinch, on the house."

THAT NIGHT SHELBY watched TV until late, but couldn't focus on anything. Because Jace was everywhere around her.

He was in the Christmas tree and the ornaments that hung on it, he was in the flames in the hearth that warmed the room in the late December chill. He was in the tin of cookies she glumly nibbled on. Outside, he was in the bicycle leaning up against the front porch railing and in the antenna on her roof.

She should have made him take the TV and bike back—

moreover, she never should have accepted them, or any of this, in the first place. But the cold, hard truth was that they made her life easier and she wasn't even sure how she'd realistically get by without the bicycle now. It had become like a lifeline to the outside world, even when the outside world was only the tiny town of Sassafras. The TV was a lifeline, too—albeit in a different way.

When she finally gave up and went to bed, Jace was in the sheets—the very smell of him lingered there. Or maybe she was imagining that, but it hardly mattered. And he was in the mistletoe that hung in the window. A mere glimpse of it flooded her senses with memories, sensations, of him kissing his way down her body.

And the mistletoe outside the front door—which had miraculously survived the storm—had provided the impetus for their first kiss.

I *should probably throw the stupid mistletoe away. It'll always remind me of him now—forever, the rest of my life.* And yet, somehow, she couldn't. She'd sent him away and knew it was best—but maybe she wasn't ready to send away her every memory of him just yet.

The truth was—she wasn't afraid of Jace. In her heart of hearts, she knew he wasn't Craig, wasn't anything *like* Craig. But he'd made her feel foolish, and incapable, and dependent. And if she was ever going to get over the things Craig had done to her, she had to feel the *opposite* of those things; she had to have the freedom to prove she could take care of herself in every way.

Sleep came with difficulty. The house seemed too quiet, and every sound from the swamp startled her awake. What she wouldn't give for some rain on her tin roof right now.

The next day she dragged herself unhappily up the beach and into Salty Pete's. She moved slowly, and her limbs felt heavy. Her *soul* felt heavy. She hadn't felt this way since just after her mother's death. *You keep trying. You keep getting back up when life knocks you down. But maybe you're just finally out of energy.*

"What's got you so Scroogy today?" Pete asked as she somberly tied on the small canvas apron where she kept straws, ink pens, and her order pad.

She shot him a look. "You're *always* Scroogy. Can't I have *one* day?"

Pete drew back slightly, clearly surprised by the retort. "Didn't say you couldn't be that way—just asked ya why."

She didn't particularly want to discuss her love life with Pete, so just said, "It's personal."

"Heard ya broke up with Jason Rose."

She lifted her head, stunned. She and Jace had barely had time to become a couple, so she thought "broke up" was a strong term, but the bigger issue was, "From who?"

"He was drowning his sorrows last night at the Rose Tavern. Small town. Word gets around."

Great. She'd come here to keep a low profile, but suddenly everyone in town knew about her by way of Jace licking his wounds?

"Well, sounds like you already know what's wrong with me then."

"Your decision or his?"

She'd dropped her gaze, but now raised it back. Suddenly Pete was talkative *and* nosy? Her lucky day.

And she still didn't care to discuss it, but maybe it would be easier to just give the old man what he wanted and get it over with—then she could go back to sulking. "Mine."

"How come?"

She just blinked. The nosy nerve of him.

But whatever. *Just answer him and be done with it.* Lunch customers would start drifting in anytime now.

"He made things move too fast. Didn't respect my independence. I just *left* a controlling relationship and I don't need to be in another one."

At this, Pete gave a short, acceptant nod. "Guess ya gotta do what ya gotta do."

Good. That was more like it.

"For what it's worth, though," he added, "Jace is a decent fella. And I don't recall a woman ever driving him to drink before, so he musta liked you a lot."

She took that in, let it settle heavily inside her. She knew his affection for her was real, same as hers for him. She didn't like that either of them was hurting. But a clean break was the only way she could truly protect herself.

"Pete's right—I ain't never seen him like that."

They both looked up to see Lonna, who'd just walked in, despite that she didn't work today. "Left my sweater last night," she said, pointing under the bar as she answered the unasked question. Stepping behind the counter, she snatched up a gray cardigan and got back to the subject of Jace. "I met a friend for a drink last night, and Jace was dragging himself outta the Rose Tavern, looking like he'd lost his best friend. He really is a nice guy. Ladies' man for sure, right? But... maybe you're the one to make him settle down."

It was time for Shelby to make herself clear. "Oh-ho-ho no—I'm not settling down with Jace, or anyone, for a very long time. The rest of the ladies can have him."

AT HOME LATE THAT AFTERNOON, she realized Christmas was almost here—and that it didn't matter at all. It made her feel lonely that this Christmas she truly had nothing to do and it would be just another day.

If things hadn't fallen apart with Jace, that would be different. Sure, she'd been nervous about the idea of meeting his family, but it had been nice knowing she wouldn't be alone, that she'd be part of a celebration, that she'd be with someone who'd begun to care about her.

Yet plenty of people the world over spent Christmas alone—it was no big deal. Soon enough the holidays would be past and life would go on. And she'd do well to get back to thinking about the future—inexpensive ways to fix up the house, saving for a cheap used car, and once she got a car she should start looking for a higher-paying job. Despite the convenience of Salty Pete's, she'd known from the start that she couldn't work there forever if she didn't want to live paycheck to paycheck.

And then an idea hit her.

Cookies.

It wouldn't be the most practical way to spend her money, but it was Christmastime and she was going to make cookies. She was going to make them for Pete. And for Lonna. And for Delia. And for the ladies at the library. Just as she and her mother had done, she would make cookies for the people in her life to thank them for their kindness.

She checked the kitchen, pleased to find old but usable cookie sheets, mixing bowls, and a rolling pin among the things Uncle Gary had left here. Paydirt. Then she glanced at the clock. If she hurried, she could get to the market and back before dark. Thank goodness she'd brought her mom's old recipe box from Chicago—one treasured thing Craig hadn't managed to somehow strip away from her.

When she walked into Delia's a little while later, the other woman wore a sheepish expression. "Shelby, I'm so sorry about what happened with—"

"It's okay," Shelby cut her off with a small smile. "It wasn't your fault—it's all on Jace. And I need to make some cookies, so point me to your baking stuff."

Delia visibly relaxed, clearly relieved Shelby wasn't holding a grudge.

Soon enough, she'd gathered up flour, sugar, vanilla, cream of tartar, powdered confectioner's sugar, food coloring, and a set of four holiday-shaped cookie cutters, the mission reviving her a little. It would feel good to do a little something for people who'd done good things for her.

Of course, that list would include Jace. But a gift of cookies to *him* might suggest she was hinting for more, trying to reopen that door—so he'd have to survive on his mother's baked goods this holiday season.

As she loaded everything from the basket up onto the checkout counter, she said to Delia, "Full price today, okay?"

"Of course." Delia looked embarrassed again, but Shelby had needed to make sure.

A few minutes later, she was pedaling home. Skies were an overcast gray-white today—no sun to draw gators out onto the road—so the ride was peaceful if chilly, making her glad she'd tossed on a light jacket for the ride. She arrived back at the cottage just as dusk dimmed the air.

After a quick sandwich for dinner, she got to work on her baking project. She turned the TV on in the other room, listening to it for company as she worked, and soon the cottage was filled with the scent of fresh-baked butter cookies. By the time she was smoothing green icing on tree-shaped cookies and yellow on stars, her shoulders ached, but it was a *satisfied* ache.

She turned in earlier than usual, tired from the baking and anticipating a good night's sleep. Tomorrow she'd package her cookies up in the inexpensive containers she'd also bought, and make her deliveries as time permitted over the next couple of days. She closed her eyes pleased that she'd created her own little version of Christmas after all.

Of course, Jace remained on her mind. It would be a

while before he wasn't there. Even as tired as she was, her body longed for his touch. She'd only been with him a few times, but it was hard to imagine connecting that perfectly with another man. Maybe she never would. Maybe she'd have to settle for memories. She'd done a lot of settling lately —she was getting used to it.

Think about cookies, not Jace. Think about cookies, not Jace. Think about cookies, not Jace. She let the mantra take her into slumber.

SHE JERKED awake with no idea how long she'd been asleep. *What was that sound?*

A vehicle? Yes, an engine, outside.

Her heart beat too hard. It was hard to think, process— but it didn't sound like Jace's truck.

Then it went quiet. And a car door slammed.

Don't panic, don't panic. There's some explanation for this.

But she didn't believe her own thoughts, not a bit, and stark fear pushed her upright in bed. Because who the hell could be out there? And if it wasn't Jace, she wasn't safe.

When she heard the front door jolt open, a cold, icy terror gripped her, freezing her in place. Why hadn't she let Jace change the lock? Why had she decided to be so damned independent at that particular moment?

Then a deep voice echoed through the cottage from down the hall. "Shelby? Shelby, are you here? It's time to come home where you belong."

Her stomach dropped. Craig. He'd found her.

CHAPTER SIXTEEN

*S*he couldn't make a sound, didn't even let herself breathe. Though that was partly from fear.

Be rational. He probably won't just kill you on the spot.

But who knows. He might—he's a lunatic.

And even if he doesn't—she couldn't let him find her. Because at worst he would hurt her, and at best he'd force her to go with him and what would she do then? Call the cops?

Maybe. If he didn't take her phone away from her. And if he didn't charm them like he managed to do with everyone else who ever met him.

What if she never saw Jace again? Maybe that was what she'd thought she wanted—but now she knew she didn't. What if she never got to make things right with him? Crazy that he would be on her mind right now—but there he was.

"Shelby, baby, where are you?"

Craig's voice came low, almost as if he was talking to himself. Then again, it was the middle of the night, when he should expect her to be asleep, so maybe it *was* mindless murmurings.

Nonetheless, she'd never heard a more paralyzing sound than his deep, even voice. He sounded so...satisfied. Smug even. Because he'd found her.

But this wasn't over. It wasn't over by a long shot. *So quit being so damn paralyzed and think.* She hadn't come this far to be drawn back into Craig's web.

Heart pounding in her chest, she silently reached over to grab her phone from the bedside table, deftly disconnecting it from the charger. Then she decided to make a move. She was going to get out of this house before he found her.

She listened, poised for action, and a moment later got the best opportunity she was going to—she heard him urinating into the toilet.

The bathroom was next to her bedroom, but closer to the front door than the back, so she moved as fast and as silently as she could, scurrying toward the back door.

Turn the lock, run out onto the little porch, make the leap into the yard.

But he was behind her—he'd heard. "Shelby! Shelby, come back here!"

She'd dashed past the corner of the house and now pressed her back up against the exterior wall, trying to breathe, trying to hide, trying to figure out her next move.

But she could hear him coming—he'd exited the cottage, too—so she couldn't stay where she was. She ran on bare feet toward the front of the house, spotting his car.

What if he'd left the keys inside? The perfect escape, but it was unlikely—and still he called her name, from just beyond where she could see, and if she opened the car door, the sound would give her away.

That was when she spotted her bicycle. Another means of escape.

But Craig could be heard striding around the house, continuing to yell for her. "You can't hide out here, Shelby.

Why are you hiding at all? I love you, baby. Now come on out and let's get out of this shithole and back where we belong."

To the unknowing, he would sound sincere. He *always* sounded sincere. But it was his actions that gave him away. And she didn't want her actions to give *her* away—and she didn't think she could reach the bike without allowing him a chance to reach *her*. So she scurried around another corner of the house, aware that she'd made almost an entire circle now—and she couldn't outrun him this way forever.

But then her eyes fell on the swamp path that led to the beach. Sure as hell not a place she'd ever been after dark, and potentially crawling with gators and God knew what else in the middle of the night—but it seemed like a safer option than endlessly trying to stay one step ahead of him in the yard.

She ran onto the path praying she stayed quiet—she tried not to ruffle any leaves and only hoped she didn't step on anything with her bare feet that would make her cry out.

When she stopped—maybe twenty yards in—she heard herself panting and only prayed the sound blended with those of the swamp. She crouched to one side, then wrapped her phone into the hem of her pajama top to hide the light—before turning it on.

She had a signal! Sometimes she did and sometimes she didn't, but right now she did!

Only then, directly to her left, she heard what she now knew to be the sound of a gator. This one was close. Too close. And yet she dared not move. She heard her heartbeat in her ears.

Just. Focus. On. The phone.

With trembling fingers, she keyed in the numbers 9-1-1.

"911—what's your emergency?"

The loudness of the woman's voice made her go tense—

what if the sound carried? She replied in the quietest of whispers. "I need help. Ex-boyfriend is chasing me."

"Does he have a weapon?"

"I don't know," she whispered—the thought a new and unsettling one. "Just please hurry. End of Cypress Stump Road."

And then she disconnected. Because she couldn't keep talking, making noise. It was too big of a risk—one she felt in her gut. Maybe it hadn't been wise—but she couldn't let Craig hear.

Her next thought—Jace. She pulled up his number and texted him feverishly: *I need help. He's here.*

Though what if he turned his phone off at night? Many people did. *She* did.

That quickly, though, the phone vibrated, delivering a reply. *On my way. Where are you?*

Hiding on path. He's in yard. Looking for me.

Stay put—I'm coming.

Shelby darkened the phone and tried to breathe.

Yet back in the yard her worst nightmare was trolling around, starting to sound still angrier that he couldn't find her. "I've been ridiculously patient, Shelby, but you're starting to piss me off. Get your ass out here, now."

And beside her the unseen alligator stirred, rustling leaves with a body that sounded heavy enough to be worrisome. Why hadn't she ever asked Jace more about gators and their behavior? Why didn't she know if she was in grave danger of being eaten by one right now?

Deep breath, deep breath. In, out. Jace is coming.

But it wasn't like he lived next door. She didn't even know *where* he lived actually—yet had the impression it was at least a ten or fifteen minute drive. And it was probably a similar distance for the police, but hopefully they were on the way as well.

When Craig's voice grew more distant—leading her to believe he'd circled to the other side of the house again—she looked to her right, on the open path, to see two dark eyes shining on her less than five feet away. Panicked, she made a radical move. She took off in another sprint. Toward her bike.

The beach would have been a safer choice—she only wished she'd realized that and kept running toward it in the first place—but now it was blocked by an alligator and she couldn't think straight.

As she hit the yard, suddenly no longer hidden by the cypresses, oaks, and other swamp foliage, she said a prayer—to God or whoever else might be up there listening. *Get me out of this safely. Get me back to Jace.*

She made it to the front of the house unseen—and then rushed to where the bike stood against the railing. It was as she climbed onto it that Craig rounded the corner of the house. "Shelby!" He ran toward her as she started rolling forward, then lunged, trying to grab onto the bike as she pedaled just beyond his reach.

"Damn it, Shelby—you bitch!"

He'd never called her a name before, and combined with his ugly tone of voice, it was as if the veil had been lifted—he'd finally let her see that ugly part of him she'd always sensed lurking beneath the surface. As she pedaled for all she was worth, she wondered if the two girlfriends he'd killed had perhaps gotten to see it, too, in their final moments.

Behind her, he gave chase, and in front of her, the swamp road appeared unfathomably dark. God, she hadn't factored this part in—it was almost impossible to see where she was going.

Then she heard his car door slam—shit, he planned to run her down in the car.

Once she was in the beams of his headlights, though, they

at least lit her way. Yet that was small consolation as she pedaled like a madwoman, desperate and tired and afraid, feeling as if she'd stepped into some kind of horror movie—because this couldn't be her real life.

Just keep pedaling. Just keep pedaling. Just keep pedaling.

Even though he was calling to her and cursing out the window. Even though the car bore down on her, too close for comfort. Even though her legs were too quickly exhausted and she wasn't even sure where she was going.

That was when she spotted more headlights up ahead, coming from the opposite direction, through the trees and around the next curve in the road. Not that it slowed the beating of her heart any—but it made her pedal harder, toward Jace.

When his headlights shone on her as well, she saw him hit the brakes, probably trying to take in what *he* saw—and then he was accelerating again, up until the two vehicles met with her in the middle, both coming to screeching halts as she skidded to a stop as well.

Both men came flying out their doors as she worked to steady the bike between her legs, her bare feet on the gravelly ground now.

"Who the hell are *you?*" Craig spat at Jace.

Before answering, Jace took a step back, reached in the bed of his pickup, and drew out a large pickaxe. "I'm your nightmare before Christmas. You picked the wrong woman to terrorize, buddy."

Just then, more engines could be heard and she realized two more vehicles—pickup trucks as well—were coming. They jerked to a halt behind Jace's truck, two more men got out, and soon one held a shovel, the other a hoe. She knew instinctively they were Jace's brothers.

The trio made a formidable sight standing in the dusty

glow of headlights, bearing garden tools as weapons. It was then that Jace glanced her way. "You okay?"

"Yeah." It came out in an exhausted whisper.

Then he looked back to Craig—who was a big guy, big enough that his size had always intimidated her—but at the moment he appeared petrified and small behind the shield of his car door.

That was when she heard sirens in the far distance.

Jace looked down at her, where she stood next to him now, and spoke quietly. "We could let him go, making it clear that if he ever comes near you again he'd have to deal with *me*. Or we can let the cops take him in and tell them everything. Might put you through a lot before it's over. But not sure there are any easy answers here. So it's your decision."

Shelby drew in her breath. Her decision. It had been a very long time since someone she cared about gave her a choice—about much of anything. But Jace had, now, about how this would go down.

And God knew she wished the nightmare could just be over. But maybe it never would be if she didn't do the hard thing here. "I want him arrested. I want to tell them about his dead girlfriends. I want him put away."

Despite that she'd spoken softly, Craig had heard, and looked shaken at the mention of dead girlfriends—almost even panicked. And for Shelby, it was confirmation. He'd done it. She'd known it in her heart, but now no doubt remained.

Tell you what, asshole," Jace said to Craig. "I'd love to beat you to a pulp for everything you've done—but it'll be simpler, and a lot less messy, to just let the cops take care of you."

"Let me by," Craig said, "and you'll never see me again. We'll call things square."

Shelby didn't wait for Jace or his brothers to reply—she

spoke boldly. "Nothing here is square, or fair, Craig. You're going to get what you deserve, once and for all."

When two police cars came racing up behind where the other vehicles were parked on the road, Craig took off running through the trees into the swamp. As the cops exited their cruisers, Rick and Tanner rushed to meet them, pointing the way, and they gave chase on foot.

Meanwhile, still in the glow of headlights but somehow feeling blessedly secluded, Shelby let Jace pull her close. Nothing had ever felt better than his strong embrace did right now.

"Thank you for coming," she breathed, weary.

He held her tight. "Are you kidding? Of course I came. I mean—honey, if he had hurt you..." He stopped, shook his head, as if the thought was too much to bear. "Or if he'd somehow toted you back up to Chicago...well, if he'd done that, he'd have ended up with three brothers bearing axes and hoes at the front door of that fancy high-rise condo."

"Do the Rose brothers always use gardening implements as weapons?" she asked with a small, tired smile.

He shrugged. "When you're raised running a nursery, guess they're the first thing you reach for."

Just then, the two police officers emerged back onto the road nearby—one of them pushing Craig along in front of him in handcuffs.

"That didn't take long," the younger looking Rose brother said.

The policeman escorting Craig replied. "Guy ran head-on into a big gator—when it was the gator or us, he started whining like a baby."

"I can't believe those alligators are actually coming in handy," Shelby murmured, stunned.

Within a few minutes, Craig sat in the back of a police cruiser, and Shelby had given a short statement. The officers told her she could go home tonight, but would need to come to the station in the morning. And while she knew it might be the beginning of something long and unpleasant, at the same time she knew it was the end of something much worse.

Just then, the taller, darker of the brothers—Rick, who she'd seen at the tavern—walked up. "Listen, why don't you take her on home?" he suggested to Jace. "They're waiting for a tow truck to take the car away—Tanner and I can hang out here until it's all wrapped up, and I'll toss the bike in my truck before we go, too."

Jace nodded. "Thanks, man."

And Shelby felt the need to add something as well, so she said to Rick, "Thank you so much. And I'm so sorry this is how we're meeting."

His brother shrugged. "Maybe we'll meet under better circumstances soon," he said. "I'm Rick, by the way."

"I'm—"

"Shelby, I know. Either that or we've saved the wrong girl."

A light laugh escaped her when she least expected it.

"I'll let you get home now, get cleaned up, and get some rest."

Jace offered a nod to his older brother, then he and Shelby got into his truck, which he eased past Craig's car without driving into the swamp, then headed toward the cottage. "For some reason," she heard herself saying unplanned, "when he broke in, my first thought was of you."

"Because you didn't let me change the lock?" he asked with a playful grin.

"That actually crossed my mind," she confessed, "but no. It was because…" She couldn't find the words she sought. *Because you make me feel safe. You make me smile. You make me*

173

want to be around you. And back there on the road with Craig, you even made me feel...capable, strong.

"Because...like it or not, you love me," he finished for her as he drove, sounding just a tad arrogant.

But it was true. She loved him. Every word she'd been unable to say right now was all about loving him. And when she'd needed help, he'd been her first thought. She'd known, deep down, that he would take care of her. And maybe that was okay—at least sometimes. He still had some learning to do about when to push and when to let her have her independence—but he wasn't Craig. He *was* her knight in shining armor. And she was suddenly thankful she had one.

Even if she didn't know what would happen between them now.

CHAPTER SEVENTEEN

*S*he walked in the cottage realizing she was a mess. Wearing short pajamas, her arms and legs had gotten scratched—and her feet were filthy, with a few cuts. She found leaves in her hair.

She showered, let Jace help her put antibiotic ointment on her cuts and scrapes, then donned fresh pajamas even though dawn was breaking out eastern-facing windows by then.

They sat by the Christmas tree, talking and cuddling on the couch.

"I'm sorry I ever compared you to him," she said. "That was awful of me."

"He messed with your head. And you were trying to get me to go away. And...I guess I can see now why some of the things I did made you feel worse instead of better, even if I meant well." He leaned over, kissed her forehead. "But I propose a fresh start. We just put all this ugly stuff behind us. I'll be completely honest with you about everything, right down to your grocery bill, and I'll work like hell to respect your boundaries. I mess up on that, you let me know. I'll do things right this time—I promise."

She drew in her breath, feeling a little guilty. "You did a *lot* of things right—a lot of things most women would love. I just wasn't ready for them. I'm sorry I wasn't more grateful because the last few weeks would have been infinitely harder without your pushy generosity."

They both smiled, and he said, "I think we're finally getting on the same page here."

And the thought of being grateful propelled her up from the couch and into the kitchen. Despite all that had happened since last night, her cookies remained on the counter, undisturbed. She carried a white snowman-shaped one back to Jace. "I made Christmas cookies. To say thank you to everyone who's helped me in some way since I came to Sassafras."

He took a big bite. "Mmm. Damn, honey, these rival my mom's." Then he winked. "But I'll deny to the death that I ever said that." Then he finished the cookie. "And hate to tell you this, but good as that was, cookies aren't gonna cut it as a thank you."

"No?" she asked, lowering her chin playfully.

"No." He reached up, pulling her onto his lap so that she was straddling him. "I can think of far better ways you can show me your appreciation."

"I can, too." Twining her arms around his neck, she leaned in for a long, deep kiss she felt everywhere. It was hard to believe she'd had the strength to send this man away. Thank God he was back. "After I've recovered a little," she added then, pulling back just slightly.

The truth was, even amid her exhaustion, he had the ability to excite her with just a touch, with just the sexy look in his eye—but she'd been through a lot, her muscles were sore, and they'd both been up since around three a.m. "Fair enough," he said. "I'm pooped, too. But I'm holding you to it."

"You won't have to—trust me. I want you more than I've ever wanted any other man, Jason Rose."

"That's what I like to hear, Shelby Scott."

He kissed her again and they eased back into snuggling.

"I'm so damn glad, honey, that we're getting this all worked out. I don't like to admit this, but…I felt lost without you."

She bit her lip, peered up at him from beneath shaded lids. "Same here." Though then she sat up a bit. "About those boundaries, though…"

"What about them?" He sounded worried.

"Well, I hope you know I still can't accept big things from you."

He slumped a little, looking deflated. "Shelby, honey, you need a car. And for the tenth time, I have one I'm not using. And I'm more convinced than ever that it's unsafe for you not to have one."

Still, she argued. "But it's too big, Jace. I can't risk getting too dependent on you too fast."

"After all this? Why the hell not?"

Well, this was an unpleasant thing to have to say right now, but… "Because you might not be around forever. I mean…who knows? From what I hear, you're a real ladies' man. You could get bored with me."

At this, however, he let out a sigh. "I'm not going anywhere, Shelby."

"But what if you do? What if you change your mind? I need to be able to take care of myself."

Another sigh. "Well, if that's what you're worried about, damn it, then I guess I'm just gonna have to marry you."

She drew back, blinked. "What?"

"I want to marry you, Shelby."

She blinked again, still trying to wrap her head around what he was saying. "You want to get married, Jace? Really?"

"Really." He stopped, sighed, met her gaze. "Look, I know it's fast. But I know I love you. I know you've turned my heart upside down and inside out like nobody I've ever met. And damn it, I want to take care of you. I know that's not PC to say these days, but it's…primal or something. And there's not a damn thing in the world wrong with a husband wanting to take care of his wife. That's what I want. To be your husband. And take care of you."

She drew in her breath, wanting to follow primal instincts of her own—yet still remembering the hell she'd just come through. "But not control me?"

"Hell no. I just want to make you happy. I want you to feel secure, to know I'll be here for you—and I want to know you'll be there for me, too."

She drew in her breath, let it back out. "What if I want a job?"

"Great. I'm comfortable financially, but who can't use more money?"

"Well, what if I want kids? Or *don't* want kids?"

"We'll figure out what's best for us."

"What if I want to have a girls' night out? If I ever make any friends."

"Then I'll hold your hair back when you throw up afterward."

"And you don't have any secrets? Like dead girlfriends?"

"Nope. Biggest problem with me is that you might worry when I start racing. 'Cause Rick, Tanner, and I are buying Rowdy's car together and I'm gonna drive it on dirt tracks."

She gasped her surprise. "That's so great, Jace! I mean—okay, yes, terrifying, and you're right, I'll worry. But I'll also love it that you're doing something that makes you happy."

His eyebrows shot up. "Is that a yes? To my proposal?"

"Was that a proposal?" she questioned, tilting her head. "I mean, seriously, Jace—you didn't actually even ask."

"You're right," he said. Then maneuvered his body out from under hers, stood up, and promptly dropped to one knee. "How's this for official, honey? Shelby Scott, who finally told me her last name, will you make me the happiest damn guy in South Carolina by marrying me?"

"Yes!"

"And letting me buy you a damn car already?"

She laughed. "Well…okay, yes."

EPILOGUE

*O*n Christmas Eve, Shelby called Uncle Gary to wish him a merry Christmas. He was her only remaining family and she wanted to start forming a stronger bond with him. And as they talked, she discovered it was her uncle who'd unwittingly told Craig where she was. Craig had found Gary in her social media, contacted him, and poured on the charm as he always did. Uncle Gary felt terrible when Shelby explained the whole situation—but she absolved him, realizing she probably should have confided in him at the beginning. She understood now that she no longer had to be afraid of everyone, that it was okay to trust in good people.

Of course, the last couple of days had held some less bright spots, as well. Giving her statement to the police, having to relive her time with Craig in stark detail. But there were also huge upsides. As a result, the family of one of Craig's deceased exes had decided to press murder charges against him and the other was considering it. Shelby, too, had pressed charges against him: breaking and entering, holding her against her will, and a host of others. She would eventually get her stuff back—both belongings and money.

There would be trials—in the plural—and that wouldn't be pleasant. But it would be worth it to watch him get what he deserved, and to make sure he couldn't do this to anyone else. And standing up against him, having the courage to do that, was adding to her renewed sense of strength.

That night, Jace took her to his family's Christmas celebration, and nothing could have done a better job of taking the bad stuff off her mind. Especially when she emptied a small red velvet stocking with her name on it to find a gorgeous diamond engagement ring inside. She'd worried the Roses might think it all seemed too fast, but instead the whole family welcomed her, and Rick even kissed her on the cheek. A very different sort of Christmas for her, yes. But not in the way she'd expected. This Christmas held new love, new hope, and a whole new family.

Afterward, Jace brought her home and they sat beside the Christmas tree, next to a roaring fire, nibbling on Christmas cookies and fudge brought home from the gathering. She peered over at him in the glow and said, "I'm pretty sure you're the man my mother kept telling me I'd find."

"I'm *completely* sure of that, honey. I'm only sorry I didn't get to meet her."

"I kinda feel her here, though—in the house," she said. "Is that crazy?"

"No," he said. "Not at all."

"Which means, you know," she said with a half smile, "that we can't get rid of this dump."

"I already knew that. I was thinking we'll buy it instead. From your uncle. We'll fix it up, make it a home. Live here together. Raise a family. It'll always be a safe place. Like it was for your mom. And a hidden little retreat. Like it's been for you."

When she awoke the next morning, he told her he had a surprise and instructed her to stay in bed until he called her.

Half an hour later, she walked into the kitchen to hear Jace say, "Ta da! I made snow toast."

Before her on the old Formica table set two plates of French toast covered with powdered sugar.

"Our first new tradition," he told her, the gesture touching her deeply. "And there'll be lots of others."

"Let's always have angels on our tree," she suggested.

"And take cookies to people in the community, like you and your mom did."

"And let's always have mistletoe all through the house."

That was when he reached up, drew down a clump of it hanging from a ribbon in the kitchen window, held it over her head and kissed her. Soon enough, he'd abandoned the white berries, the snow toast sat forgotten, and he was easing his hands up under the nightshirt she wore.

"Jace, it's Christmas," she reminded him.

"Sex on Christmas," he said. "That's another good tradition."

❄

Other Titles

Wildest Dreams

The Red Diary

Letters to a Secret Lover

Tempt Me Tonight

Swept Away

The Weekend Wife

The Bewitching Hour

The Guy Next Door

The Cinderella Scheme

ABOUT THE AUTHOR

Toni Blake's love of writing began when she won an essay contest in the fifth grade. Soon after, she penned her first novel, nineteen notebook pages long. Since then, Toni has become a RITA™-nominated author of more than twenty contemporary romance novels, her books have received the National Readers Choice Award and Bookseller's Best Award, and her work has been excerpted in *Cosmo*. Toni lives in the Midwest and enjoys traveling, crafts, and spending time outdoors.

Learn more about Toni and her books at:
www.toniblake.com

Made in the USA
Monee, IL
26 April 2023